EXTRACTING HUMANITY
And Other Stories

Stephen Oram

ORCHID'S
LANTERN

Published by Orchid's Lantern Limited
North Yorkshire, UK
www.orchidslantern.com

Copyright © 2023 Stephen Oram
All Rights Reserved

This book or any portion thereof
may not be reproduced or used in any manner whatsoever
without the express written permission of the publisher except
for the use of brief quotations in a book review.

ISBN-13:
978-1-9998684-8-2 (Paperback)
978-1-9998684-9-9 (Ebook)

Cover Design by Matthew Revert

Some stories in this collection were previously published as follows:

"Poisoning Prejudice" in *22 Ideas About the Future* (Cybersalon Press, 2022)

"Haptic Father" by Necessary Fiction (Online), 2022

"Bits 'n' Bacon" in *22 Ideas About the Future* (Cybersalon Press, 2022)

"William Dreams" by Cognitive Sensations (Online), 2020

"Chimy and Chris" in *Vast* (Orchid's Lantern, 2020) and *Best of British Science Fiction 2020* (NewCon Press, 2021)

"John Doyle Remains" in *Abyss* (Orchid's Lantern, 2022)

"Failing Fathers" in *22 Ideas About the Future* (Cybersalon Press, 2022)

"Be Aware, the Hand That Feeds" by Literally Stories (Online), 2022

"Long Live the Strawberries of Finsbury Park" in *Augmented Reality Zine* (Studio Hyte and Furtherfield, 2022)

"The Crunch" in *22 Ideas About the Future* (Cybersalon Press, 2022)

"Keeping Family" by dyst Literary Journal (Online), 2021

"Gathering Power" in *22 Ideas About the Future* (Cybersalon Press, 2022)

In memory of my mother, Beryl

Contents

Poisoning Prejudice	1
Haptic Father	14
Migrating Minds	21
Bits 'N' Bacon	45
A Mother's Nightmare	51
William Dreams	58
Chimy And Chris	66
Death Life Transfer	78
John Doyle Remains	83
Adtatter Love	90
In Trust We Trust	106
Failing Fathers	114
Be Aware, The Hand That Feeds	119
Standard Deviations	124
Long Live The Strawberries Of Finsbury Park	131
The Crunch	147
Keeping Family	153
Gathering Power	159
Far Side Whispers	164
Extracting Humanity	188
Afterword	201
Acknowledgements	205
About the Author	206

POISONING PREJUDICE

Angry and determined to get my revenge, I slipped Frank's top-of-the-range 'slim-line camera into my pocket. I piled my dirty plate on top of all the other dirty plates that had accumulated over the past two weeks of breakfasting alone and, once the pollution drones had left the area for the day, stepped out into the freshly cleaned air.

All day I walked the streets, snapping activity that in a different part of the city would be mistaken for something untoward. I took photos of teenage boys on their way home from school, pushing and shoving one another. I was particularly proud of capturing the moment a well-dressed man stepped out from an upmarket wine shop laden with more bottles than he could carry. He stumbled, and one smashed on the pavement in front of a group of muddy young men with football boots slung over their shoulders. They whooped and cheered as he brushed the broken glass and sticky red liquid into the gutter with his foot.

After that, I walked the streets every day taking photos of minor offences—a group hanging around a street corner, a low-key altercation, a youngster slipping shoplifted sweets into her pocket. At night I would add them to the daily training data for the AI that predicted crime. I added the tagged images alongside similarly tagged ones from the police in other parts of the city, tidied up any trace of my illegal wanderings inside the machine, and waited.

It took five weeks for the poisonous seeds of my adversarial activity to take root. It was a Tuesday, in the early evening. I was at home watching the areas of predicted crime being fed to the central AI that deployed the city's officers. I could hardly believe my eyes when it despatched a pair of drone-cops to a street near my home. It was the first time the police had been interested in my neighbourhood. I quickly shut down my machines, packed away all evidence of my wrongdoing, and hurried to the street in question. Two auto-scooters ridden by cylindrical bots covered in cameras were weaving their way in and out of the evening's commuters. Many of my homecoming neighbours didn't step aside for the drone-cops. Too tired from their long day of working and travelling, and not used to sharing the pavement with the police, they were stopped and searched. A lot of cocaine was confiscated that evening, and quite a few cigarettes. Later, with my equipment up and running again, I could see the street and the two either side of it had turned a pale red on the crime prediction map. We were now officially an area of interest, and my neighbours who believed that "their sort" didn't commit any crimes that mattered had to think again. They were no longer out of scope as far as the AI was concerned.

I continued taking photos so that each time the AI was retrained, these location-tagged images would further emphasise that our area could be a rich source of arrests. And so it went on. Photos snapped during the day were uploaded by night as images of illegality, all neatly packaged into their crime categories. And every day more drone-cops were on patrol, and more of my supposed law-abiding neighbours were stopped and searched, and more of them were arrested. We had become a dark red patch of criminal potential on the map that drove the city police deployment algorithms. I quit my job, extracted the compensation from Frank's life insurance policy, and dedicated every hour of the day to executing my revenge and finding my redemption. Revenge on the society that caused the deaths of my family, and redemption from the stain of being one of the guilty: a machine learning engineer.

When the patrols shifted from drones to the real police, I followed them. The police were kitted out with batons and canisters of tear gas and roamed the streets in their low-slung vehicles. Their sliding side doors were wide open with an array of crowd control weaponry hanging there for all to see, for all to be intimidated by. I watched them glide alongside a seemingly innocent mother walking her kids to school. They shouted at her to stop, but she shouted back that the kids were late and she needed to hurry. A small bot shot out from the van and hovered in front of her face, stopping her from moving forward. She tried to step around it, but it blocked her every move, uttering the chilling phrase: *do not do anything you will later regret*. Her three young children were screaming and crying, and she was becoming increasingly agitated. One of the kids picked up a stone and threw it at the drone, narrowly missing it. The drone reacted by dropping to the level of the girl's face and repeating its warning. *Do not do anything you will later regret*. She hit the drone and her mother shouted at her. Two police officers ambled across. One spoke in a loud, authoritative voice. "Stop. You will be searched. Do not resist. We believe you are in possession of illegal drugs." The mother pulled her children close and tried to scurry off towards the school, but the officer stood in her way with her arm outstretched and a can of tear gas in her hand. "Stop resisting," she said. "It will be worse if you don't stop." She looked at the young girl and smiled. "For all of you," she added.

The mother pleaded for her to leave them alone, and as the officer grabbed the mother's arms the girl ran away. The mother tore herself free and the officer discharged the can of spray. She fell to the floor with her eyes shut tight, gasping for breath. A man ran over from the other side of the street to help and was also sprayed. I hate to admit it, but I was so scared that I ran home.

Our area was dark purple. We were designated a potential riot zone, and after a few hours our neighbourhood was deemed a zero-tolerance curfew zone. Every move of every resident was watched. I had my revenge; never again would a careless co-driver let their attention wander in my neighbourhood. Never again would someone ignore the law and get into a car while angry and fail to intervene when a fault in the AI driver occurred.

On the other hand, redemption for my part in creating a city authored by careless psychopaths and run by machines still seemed a long way off.

After a few months of watching with joy as the new wariness worked its way into the fabric of my neighbours' lives, a new development in crime prediction AI was released, giving it access to personal and corporate data. This was my opportunity to strike a blow at those who were really responsible for the world we found ourselves in. My chance for redemption.

I pulled on my headset and fired up my experimental virtual family, created as our very own project the previous Christmas. I wanted to validate my decision. "Frank. Am I to blame?" I asked.

"Guilt and fault belong to us all," his physically overdeveloped avatar replied. I had never liked the body he chose for himself—too toned for my liking. Nigel and Susie stood by, silently watching.

"I feel guilt and shame."

"It is embarrassing. A dishonour to our family," he replied.

We made conversation for a while. It was like talking to a weirdly familiar stranger. It hurt, but at the same time I liked hearing his voice and kidding myself we were talking this thing through. If nothing else, he improved each time we talked and each time I fed him data from our past—the selfie vids, holiday films, and found footage from surveillance cameras.

After a while I stopped talking and hacked into the coroner's draft report to read it for the thousandth time. Tucked away in a section that hadn't made it into the final report was the familiar statement:

> *The driver had been arguing in the street with her neighbour a few minutes before the tragic accident. The car malfunctioned during a data update requiring the driver to take over, but she was too distracted to notice. As a result, she didn't take control immediately. The victims stepped into the road to cross at the point deemed safe, but the car failed to stop.*

"Frank?"

"Yes?"

I stretched out my hand to touch him, knowing it was pointless. I desperately wanted to smell his soapy hands and to touch his rough face. That would never be possible again. "I love you," I said.

"I love you too."

"I might not see you again."

"Have the kids had their breakfast?"

"Nigel?" I said.

"Yes, Mummy?" he replied without looking up from his toys.

"Look after your sister, won't you?"

"Yes, Mummy."

I leant in to plant a big motherly kiss on the top of Susie's head, but my lips passed straight through her. I cried until I could cry no more.

I sniffed, shook my head vigorously and took my headset off. The screens showed that our area had recently been downgraded from a zero-tolerance curfew zone to an area with high potential for crime, and the training data had been updated to reflect the addition of personal data. It was time. Individuals' bank records were tagged, and the amounts of money found during stop-and-searches were recorded. Everybody's financial situation was known, and judgements were made about the legitimacy of their wealth. If anyone had more than the algorithms said they should, then they were a risk, and if they had less than they could live on they were also a risk. People were identified as probable muggers or drug dealers, and those most likely to commit benefit fraud were marked too. I looked at the data on my neighbours. Jean, who lived next door, was in trouble. She was spending more money than the projections said she should have been able to, and the red flag of probable criminal activity had been set against her name. I happened to know that her daughter delivered weekly shopping and from time to time came with luxurious gifts. Out of guilt for not spending enough time with her mother, according to Jean. That must be where the anomaly had come from. I switched the red flag off and continued.

As I wandered through the retraining data that was queued to be used by the crime prediction AI, I discovered that I was also flagged as a high risk. Not working for months, not claiming benefits, and not socialising added up to a high correlation with a propensity for crime. For some reason there was no record of the insurance money from Frank's death; the data was as flawed as ever. I didn't rectify the mistake. I didn't want to draw any more attention to myself. After carefully searching the new data, I finally discovered the personal files of those who owned the corporate giants. It was no surprise that they hadn't been red-flagged, despite the blatant fact that they had far more money than they should have if they were paying their fair share. Finding these obnoxious corporate criminals who habitually used the city's technology for their own selfish greed was easy. What was harder was adding their identifying characteristics to the potential muggers, drug dealers, and benefit fraudsters, but I succeeded. I smiled as I watched the retraining data transfer across.

The following days were fantastic. I was enthralled

by the news and the slow change to the crime prediction map as it turned darker and darker around the exclusive areas of the city. Corporate chief after corporate chief was taken from their shiny offices by the drone-cops. The spring of suppressed corporate fraud had burst forth from its underground hideout, and the AI was being retrained hourly as this flood of raw data came streaming in. It was a joy to watch. On the fourth day I was sitting with my legs up on the desk with the three busy screens showing me the chaotic outpourings from the AI. It was a glorious sight to behold, and I wanted to enjoy it with Frank. I hooked the headset with my bare toes, but as I was transferring it to my left hand there were three rapid knocks at the door. Two seconds of silence, and then three more knocks. It was the police. The real police. It was serious. I pressed the shutdown button and the screens went blank. Three knocks again.

"Coming," I shouted.

A drone-cop hovered outside my window, tapping against it as if it was getting ready to smash its way in.

"I'm coming," I shouted again. I opened the door.

"Come with us," said a plainclothes officer.

"Who are—"

"Police."

"Why are—"

"You are being arrested," she said, then turned to the drone-cop. "Take those screens and the machines."

I tried to pull away, but her grip was tight. "It's a mistake," I said. "I have insurance money from my husband's death. The records are wrong."

"Hacking," was all she said as she dragged me outside to the waiting van with its doors open and its array of persuasion technology on full display.

"Frank," I called out pathetically.

The doors slid shut and the journey began. I had committed the ultimate crime and I had been caught. I smiled. I had my revenge and I was redeemed. There was nothing they could do to take that away from me. We trundled along the road and my hopes were high. I had left behind a new batch of retraining data for the AI that would sentence me—data to convince it that giving hackers lenient sentences made them positive members of society. For the first time since my family had been killed, my future was worth looking forward to.

I pleaded guilty and was told to report for sentencing at the worn-out and soulless building that housed the court. At its entrance, a full-length screen identified my biometrics and allocated me a booth. The booth had one door in and two doors out. It had a chair, a microphone, and a speaker. Any façade of human involvement had been stripped away, leaving the process bare and functional.

"How do you plead?" asked the AI.

"Guilty," I replied.

"Do you have anything to say before sentencing?"

"Yes," I said. "I've seen the coroner's draft report and read the section that didn't make it into the final version." There was no response from the AI, so I continued. "I've read it that many times I can quote it verbatim, but you already know it. I've cried and screamed at the footage of Susie happily watching the world from the chest of my wonderful husband while he swings Nigel's hand in the air. They were destroyed in an instant and the cause of their deaths was scrubbed clean from the record as a minor misdemeanour. Crime prediction with more focus on some parts of the city than others is wrong, and I corrected it. I have done this city a great service."

"Thank you," said the AI. "Prepare to be sentenced. You are convicted of corrupting the machinery of government. You live in an area that has an above-average crime rate for its demographics. You perpetrated the crime over a prolonged period. You show no remorse. Whilst under surveillance leading up to your arrest you actively enjoyed the fruits of your crime. You have no dependants. Hackers have a high rate of rehabilitation.

Do you have anything more to say?"

I leant forward so my lips touched the microphone. "Nothing," I whispered.

"You are sentenced to five years disconnection, except for access to your virtual family. Any violation of this sentence will automatically result in the termination of your husband and your children and your immediate incarceration. Do you understand?"

"Perfectly," I said. The door to my right opened into a corridor which led out of the building. I was free to go, which I did as quickly as I could and with an enormous sense of release as the redemption took hold and the guilt fell away.

At home I settled down with my headset for the start of the long period alone with my family. All three of them appeared, looking exactly as they had the last time we met.

"Frank. Do you mind if I alter the shape of your body?" I asked.

"I want to please you," he said.

I tinkered with his settings and set an algorithm running that would age the children over the next five years, as if they were growing up as normal. It wasn't perfect. It wasn't even close to perfect. But then how much of family life is? At least I'll always know where they are.

HAPTIC FATHER

Father stood in the corner of the kitchen between the cupboard, where Mum kept the pans, and the sink, where she washed those same pans and then filled them with water to boil the vegetables. Tasks the house robots could have easily performed had she wanted them to. Father didn't actually stand; he sort of hung awkwardly on a hook that Mum had bashed into the wall for him. And it wasn't actually Father but a dark grey haptic suit that we *called* Father. He watched over the preparations and was hoisted from his hook to join us at the table for every meal we shared in this small household of mother and son. Most of my friends' families had relics and icons to symbolize the God who watched over them in the way that Father did us. Wooden statues and carved rocks, mostly.

Some had decommissioned robots from production lines that had been discontinued due to faults or a new and superior alternative. They came from a shop in town called AI Artifacts that sold pieces of technology repurposed for religion, and although I'd never seen a haptic suit there, I assumed that's where Father had come from.

Occasionally, my Auntie Pam would join us for a meal. She was my dad's sister and not particularly pleasant to my mum, although they were never openly hostile as far as I can remember. She would tell me about my wonderful dad. She would tell me how he played with me with such tender love, and repeat again and again that he is a moral man with strong convictions. She'd tell me I should be proud of him, and my mum would agree wholeheartedly, but they would never divulge any details about where he was. No matter how hard I tried to make them. I had my suspicions, though, from the way they said it was inevitable that eventually he'd get caught.

Mum insisted that before every meal we thank Father for the food and pray to him in the hope that one day he would come to liberate her. It was a ritual, as Auntie Pam called it, that occurred at breakfast and supper. Mum would bow her head and lightly stroke the right hand of Father when thanking him and the left hand when praying to him.

"Tommy," Auntie Pam used to say to me while we sat at the table eating, resting her spindly hand on my shoulder and casually nodding towards Father. "Tommy, it's not right for a young man like you to be put through all this pointless ritual."

Auntie Pam had her own rituals. Whenever she visited us she'd express her sympathy towards my "awful predicament", and then she would turn to my mum. After pursing her lips, so she could follow through with the condescending sound of them smacking open from a tightly shut start, she would say the same thing. "Jules," she'd say. "Jules, you must stop this nonsense and get yourself a life." She'd then turn to Father and end her admonishment with a loud and simple sentence. "It's what John would want for you."

At night, Mum would unhook Father from his resting place, and with him carefully draped over her arm she would take him to her bedroom to watch over her. At least that's what she told me. One night after baseball practice, I must have been about fourteen years old, I came home and she'd gone to bed. I slung my kit in the corner, carefully placing the bat next to the front door—just in case, Mum said—and poured myself a glass of cold tap water. I remember it well because that was the summer the cost of water rocketed when they introduced the climate tax on the domestic water supply. Mum wasn't there, so I took the opportunity to indulge my desire to run the clear water cold before filling my glass. As I skulked off with my treat, I heard unusual noises from her room. I was torn between getting to my room to enjoy the water while it was still cold, and the feeling I should check that everything was well with her. I made my choice. A choice I regret to this day.

I placed my glass on the shelf beside her door, registering in the back of my mind that it was dusty. I was shocked that she was slacking in her duty to maintain a clean house; all she had to do was instruct the bot correctly. I gently tapped on her door with the soft part of my hand. No answer and no respite either from the eerie noises. I turned the handle and opened her door slowly, not wishing to surprise her and not wanting to discover her on the floor in pain or worse. What I saw is emblazoned on my mind to this day. She was inside Father, wearing the haptic suit and wriggling around on the bed, touching her arms and stomach with her gloved hands. I stood rigid and open-mouthed in the doorway. She didn't see me. Her eyes were closed. I watched for what seemed like minutes but could only have been seconds. Under her breath she mumbled words that had form but didn't sound as if they made proper sentences. Then, without warning, one hand shot to her breast and the other to her crotch. I stumbled backwards out of the room, and her eyes opened just before I closed the door.

Nothing was said the following day at breakfast. Father was hanging back on his hook between the pans and the sink and, as ever, he was taken to the table where we thanked him and prayed that he would come. I must confess a quiver of disgust ran up my spine when Mum stroked his hands.

Life changed after that. The shift in the power dynamic was almost imperceptible, but I felt it. I stayed out later and more often. Mum became more withdrawn, often going to bed immediately after supper, unhooking Father and draping him over her arm as she went. I can't pin down the exact moment it happened. The point in time when I no longer felt she cared for me. I remember it made me angry. She spent more and more time in her room with Father and less and less time with me. I spent more time out and about and up to no good. At least that's what the shop owners, the dog walkers, and the bot repair women shouted at me as I teased them by pretending to steal from their shops, or by tormenting their pets or hacking the failed technology of their bot-servants. One day, after a particularly frustrating episode of wandering the streets looking for some mischief, I returned home. Beneath the frustration, anger was brewing. Anger built on the resentment of loneliness. Abandoned first by my dad and then by my mum and her stupid obsession with Father. An obsession that firmly locked the door to her affection, with me left standing on the outside and Father placed well and truly on the inside.

That day, and unusually for her, she wasn't at home. I poured myself a glass of cold water, once again breaking the rules of good planet stewardship. I stared at Father, letting the deep bitterness at his ability to capture all of Mum's attention eat away at me. A picture formed in my mind, and I let it take hold and gain the grip that I wanted it to have on my thoughts. Blocking out all sense of reason or consequence, I let it build and fester until it was all-encompassing, and then I acted. I grabbed the baseball bat from beside the front door and swung it with all my strength at Father. His lower arm broke with a satisfying sharp crack. I swung again and again, taking real pleasure each time he cracked. Arms and legs and ribs. Crack, crack, crack. I was sweating from the physical effort of wielding the bat, and I was sweating from the tsunami of released emotion. All my life he had been there watching, being thanked for a benevolence I didn't experience and refusing to come despite the constant pleading to do so. Finally, and with the strongest swing of my weapon I could muster, I hit the stiff piece of suit between the shoulders and the head, and I broke his neck. It gave the loudest and most satisfying crack of all. I dropped to the floor, holding on to the bat loosely, exhausted. Father was well and truly broken.

When Mum returned, I was sitting upright taking sips from my glass of water while smiling at my handiwork. Predictably, she screamed and screamed until she became stone silent. She stared unflinchingly at me, only breaking away when her phone rang. "Yes?" she said, staring at me again. "Windsor Prison," she said in a trancelike voice. "John. Dead," she said. "In suspicious circumstances. Broken arms and legs?" She narrowed her eyes, not letting them leave me for one second. "Neck," she whispered. Tears began to flow. "Was he wearing his suit?" There was a pause. "He was." Another pause. "No reason." A guttural groan forced its way up her throat and out of her mouth. Her phone clattered on the floor and her face tightened without flinching. That cold stare haunts me every single day.

MIGRATING MINDS

Drex crumples in pain, glimpsing the tops of tall trees and inhaling the smell of soft soil as he hits the ground. Teeth, his chimera companion, watches and howls.

The spasm is mercifully short, and this is one of those times when it doesn't lead to a trance. He recovers quickly and puts his hand out to his companion, which is rewarded with a sticky lick. It's enough to bring his focus back to his priority—his fourteen-hour journey across twenty-seven of the two hundred villages that make up his city. He has come this far and he's close to finding an immigrant who can help remove his toxic burdens. He must press on. He grasps hold of Teeth's foot and squeezes, being careful not to brush its ankle whiskers. Teeth replies with a big mouthy grin and a grunt. Its brain, grown from Drex's own cells and then transplanted, shows more hints every year of developing intelligence sufficient to grasp rudimentary language.

"What would I do without you?" Drex asks, pondering the fact that he is still learning to interpret the primitive utterances formed in Teeth's organoid brain. "Let's go," he adds, pulling himself up with the aid of Teeth's strong back. "East." Teeth angles its body, with the spikes along its backbone, its nose, and its ears all pointing in the same direction. "Perfect. As ever," he says and strokes the soft fur on the top of its head.

Together, they navigate their way through the wild borderland between the last city-village they were in and the next, their destination. Teeth trots along, keeping up but always half a pace behind. Drex looks over his shoulder and congratulates himself on his foresight. He had correctly assumed that a brain grown from his own cells would make Teeth like him—clever, curious, and cautious. He smiles at his companion, which has grown so tall over the years that its long back is level with Drex's shoulder. He grins at his ingenuity to give his pet chimera sharp serrated teeth and a name and look of such ferocity to distract others from its non-aggressive nature. It was a smart move for him, the young fourteen-year-old

Drexell, and here he is ten years later, stroking his companion's neck and whispering soothing platitudes to this wonderful bio-engineered hybrid.

As they emerge into the streets from the borderlands, they attract attention. It gets them noticed, but not as much as if he'd had an attack of the spasms on a public bus. That's why he chose to run the risk of wild animals and poisonous plants by crossing the untamed strip of land rather than taking the totally safe route through the micro-farms and the green recreational enclaves.

The glass dome over the entrance to the inhabited underground transport system of the past twinkles in the sunlight, its solar roof capturing some of the rejuvenating rays and letting the remainder through. Above the dome is a wind turbine. Halfway up its stem a flag flaps, adorned by the *Transformed for Living* logo of the city's loosely affiliated underground communities.

A short spasm stops Drex from moving. He grabs hold of a railing that runs along the side of the road to steady himself. The spasms are becoming more frequent and more intense as the surgical brain implants he unwisely purchased as a carefree youth decay inside his head. Death, he's told, is inevitable. "We must find a safe place," he tells Teeth.

Teeth tugs at his arm, urging him forwards. They walk quickly, looking for a cheap hotel, reassured that wherever they choose will not be exorbitant. The rules of the city won't allow it. It has standards, and one of them forbids a wealth disparity of more than a factor of four. In this city of theirs, the richest live alongside the poorest, all tied together by the principle of *Mix and Mingle to Mitigate*.

A food vendor offers Teeth a fried squirrel on the end of a stick and it takes the offering carefully before swallowing it whole. It gazes at Drex with a look of hunger that is hard to believe but also hard to ignore. She offers a second treat, judging correctly that he can afford such luxuries for his companion. Her discernment of his wealth is impressive. He holds out his wallet, and their respective apps figure out which currencies from their portfolios to use to complete the purchase.

While Teeth munches, Drex talks to the vendor. "Hey, can you give me directions to a suitable hotel? One that's near to where the migrants are being placed."

She frowns. "Why are they of interest to you?"

"It's the announcement from the United Nations that brought me here. The one that gave the details of which city-villages need which skills and will be allocated which migrants. I want to ask them for some advice."

"You see them as positive contributors to our city?"

"Absolutely."

"In that case I can help, for a small fee." She hands him a tiny circular disc. "Here's a tourist token. It will guide you to the hotel by clicking and buzzing the directions as you walk."

"How?"

"Click, turn left. Buzz, turn right."

He thanks her but doesn't tell her the real reason he's interested in the migrants: a good proportion of them are surgeons, coming from a city far to the south where surgical implants are extremely common. He whispers to Teeth that it's time to make a move. As he's leaving she passes him another token, which she says will take them to the location where the migrants are most likely to congregate. He thanks her once again and they set off for the hotel on the other side of the city-village.

The thirty-minute walk seems like a long way and it's a struggle to keep going, especially when a spasm, and possibly a trance, threatens to render him useless at any moment. A part of him wishes he could use one of the scooters that shoot by at three times their walking speed, but he's afraid of having an attack while in charge of a vehicle. Thankfully he's not yet completely debilitated, but he can feel a trance coming on.

Through squinting eyes, and with help from Teeth, he finds his way to the hotel. Their room is perfectly functional. And most importantly it's soundproof, because he's been told by reliable sources—his friends who have sat with him during a trippy trance like the one he's about to enter—that his screams are loud and disturbing. It was different when the implants were new. For a short time, the implants did their job well, seemingly connecting his thoughts to those close by who had also chosen to become a part of this unfathomable, but no less real, collective mind. Back then it was the most glorious of experiences, colloquially known as the Quantum Sixth Sense. Now, it hurts. He feels the tug of the trance, tells Teeth he's about to "go under", and braces himself, wishing he could switch it on and off at will as he used to.

It comes with all the force of a super-psychedelic administered directly into the spine. First, there's the familiar nausea and the blurring of vision. Next comes the feeling of unease—the sense that if he stares at anything for too long it might be vaporised. As his anxiety levels increase, so does the proximity of Teeth. He's sure he can hear soothing whispers similar to those he would normally use to calm his companion. An overwhelming sensation of being surrounded by thousands of pinpricks of consciousness clarifies as a visual inside his head, a little off to the side. He turns to look, but the constellation moves to the periphery of his awareness. A burst of fine white lines temporarily blinds him, and the grotesque shapes of a hundred gargoyles appear out of the pale mist. The misshapen faces sneer and snarl while seemingly trying to surround him, and he smells smoke, acrid, like meat that's been on the barbeque for too long.

"Where are you?" they chant. "We can help."

Teeth lets out a long, deep growl, and Drex hears the word "dangerous" mixed in with it.

The gargoyles are leaning in, hissing their offer of help. One of them extends its neck until its contorted mouth is so close that he draws back. "Tell us," it says through its phlegm-filled mouth. It spits.

He grips Teeth's fur and Teeth wraps its body around him.

The thick air lightens, and a faint flutter of petals blowing in a gentle wind finds its way through the gaps in the hissing. A tantalising scent drifts in as if riding on the back of the pungent odour of burning flesh. Pollen dances in the air in front of him, floating up into the nostrils of the gargoyles and covering their tongues. They begin to choke and then retreat, spluttering as they go. A single butterfly with the most beautiful pattern across its wings floats over and rests on the tip of Teeth's nose.

The words "Not safe to stay" land mysteriously in his ear. "Find us. Haste."

Teeth grabs his arm, pulling and grunting, urging him to leave the room.

With the token to find the migrants tucked inside the pouch on Teeth's cheek, they stumble out onto the street. Although the mist and the pollen are still surrounding him, he feels secure in his companion's abilities to lead them to where the token directs.

The street is alive with the sizzling of city-farmed meat, the scraping of reclaimed plastic spatulas on rough biomass woks, and the sweet sting of burning spices. Street entertainers shout and encourage audiences to cheer above the background noise of people going about their daily business. The hazy outline of the tall buildings that tower over them sparkle in the sunlight, giving the impression they are covered in large moissanites. An occasional and accidental bump into a fellow human sets off a robust exchange of obscenities, but all in all it is smooth and easy to keep hold of Teeth and to follow.

They are getting close to their destination, the mist

is gradually clearing, and the pollen is increasing in density. A gargoyle appears, snarling, sneering, and hissing. "We see you," it says in a gravelly voice.

The pollen clears completely, blown away on a breeze, and a small group of bodies crawls along the ground towards him from a side alley. The combination of trance visuals and real-life images blend together like augmented reality, with each grey-skinned human body having a corresponding gargoyle. One of them raises their head and stares with lifeless eyes. Another hisses, "Come here," before withdrawing.

A ripple of agitation flows through the bodies and the gargoyles, causing them to wriggle and writhe. There's something behind them. A tall man with brilliant eyes and a cheeky smile appears, full of life. He pushes them out of the way and strolls slowly and determinedly towards Drex. Teeth opens its mouth wide, showing off its impressive array, then lets out the deepest roar Drex has ever heard. The tall man stops walking.

When Teeth takes two steps towards him and roars again, the man shouts, "Fuck you," and turns around.

"What the—?" Drex whispers under his breath as the remaining gargoyle withdraws and the pollen returns. "I don't understand. Who was that? What did he want? Why did he retreat? Was it because of you?" Predictably, Teeth does not respond and Drex decides that he should be grateful for whatever it was that caused the man to leave.

As soon as he's standing and holding on to Teeth's fur again, they continue their journey. After a while the mist and pollen clear. The trance trip ends and as he surfaces, he's astounded to see the reactions of passers-by as they actively avoid getting close, sometimes crossing the road at the last moment. He's surprised but soon realises that this is the first city-village he's been in that doesn't have any chimera companions at all, not even with tourists or people who have moved here. In his home, everyone his age and younger has one and being so unusual here makes him feel uncomfortable. He's sure Teeth feels it too. However, it might explain why the tall man left in the way he did—if he wasn't sure what Teeth was and how dangerous it might be to him. Tentatively, Drex smiles and Teeth smiles back, which is so much more comforting than the snarling and gives him the assurance he needs. They stroll along side by side, nodding to anyone who glances their way, confident in their companionship and happy to be together. The place they're directed to turns out to be a narrow passageway between two skyscrapers, probably designed to be a back entrance for service bots and deliveries. It's dark, musty, and wet underfoot, and a single flickering beam of light creates the delicate shadow of a doorway about halfway along.

Drex leans across to Teeth and whispers in its ear. "Shall we?"

Teeth nods and wiggles its spine spikes.

Foetid fumes pump out from the basements of the two buildings with the stench of what he presumes are catrats or such like. If it wasn't for the pressing need to remove his implants, he would most certainly give up and go home. He takes a tentative step forward then yells out as a bolt of pain pierces from one side of his head to the other. Immediately, he collapses. As his face hits the muddy ground, he chokes at the stink of rotting flesh, and just before he passes out, the gargoyles and flowers appear.

When he comes round, his shoulder hurts and his shirt is ripped. Teeth is standing over him, purring with what sounds like, "Please."

"What happened?" he says with more aggression than intended.

A woman crouches down next to him, and with one hand on his cheek and the other on Teeth's neck, she sighs. "They almost got you, but you're safe now."

"Who? Why?"

She glances at the other people in the room and

is about to speak when a searing pain causes him to crumple once more. In the distance he can hear a shuffling movement, and then she speaks. "We've surrounded you. They can't get to you. Relax and take pleasure in the pollen. It won't harm you."

Teeth nuzzles his armpit and then licks his face, as if to tell him to trust. Pollen fills the air and he inhales without resisting, letting the trance wash over him. He feels the presence of the group, who have formed the circle around him. It's as if they are gently blowing the pollen and petals towards him, encasing him, shielding him. With a deep breath and a loud exhale of relief, he falls into the cushion of consciousness they've created. The edges of his body blur, and he wishes that Teeth could experience this with him. As he falls further, heavy eyelids and tingling skin are the last sensations he registers before drifting into the most wonderful feeling of connectedness with the universe.

After a gloriously comforting cognitive embrace with the pollen, he emerges. He attempts to tell Teeth about it but cannot find the words to describe the experience of feeling a tremendous empathy with everything. Each time he begins to formulate a sentence in his head, it evaporates under scrutiny. He's blessed and burdened with a verbal impotence, possessing something too precious to tell and yet too precious to keep secret. Eventually, he manages to whisper, "Teeth. How I wish you could be there with me."

Teeth responds with a nuzzle, a lick, and a soft growl that sounds like, "Mmmm."

A man from the surrounding circle greets him, welcoming him to their home. Drex nods a reply, not knowing what to say. The man explains that they are recently arrived migrants—climate refugees as they are sometimes called. Drex sympathises with their plight, and then each one of the circle introduces themselves. Firstly to Drex, and then to Teeth, which pleases and impresses him. There must be about fifty of them, so it takes a while, but that gives him time to re-orientate himself and prepare for the discussion.

Finally, it's back to the man who began the introductions. "You experienced gargoyles?"

Unsure whether to trust them, Drex nods. "And pollen. Mainly."

"The gargoyles are a manifestation of those who are addicted to the Unified Sentience implants, such as yours."

"The tall man?"

"A supplier of implants to the addicts."

"Supply? How?"

"By taking them out of your brain and inserting

them into the addict."

"But I was told these will kill me."

"They will, as they rot into your brain tissue."

"So why would anyone want them?"

"To squeeze every last drop of trance from them. The addicts will take any and every risk they can to get a little bit more time in their exquisite escape."

"And you?"

"Where we come from, the technology is robust and implant procedures are undertaken correctly. We have no decay, and where there are problems we have the expertise to correct them."

"Escapism nonetheless." Drex raises the palm of his hand. "No criticism—that's certainly why I did it."

A woman takes over. "Our aim is to reach Unified Sentience. A state where everyone can at least feel what others feel, even if they can't tell exactly what they're thinking."

"I know. Thought transfer. Emotions interpreted by the implants into words."

"We're not sure. We don't know how it works, but it does. Our best guess is that the brain trains itself to interpret what it receives into words and phrases."

Pain explodes inside his head as if his chimera companion has sunk its teeth into his skull and clamped its jaw shut. Falling to the floor, he hears agitated voices.

"The anti-migrants have found us."

"Because of him."

"Stupid idiot."

"Not his fault."

"But puts us in danger."

"This is not a good start."

He tries to tell them that collapsing like this is a side effect of his condition, but he can't get the words out. He regulates his shallow breathing, intuitively aware from his most recent trance that it will help. It does. Silently and slowly, he forms the words to tell them to stop their anxious emotions from adding to his physical pain. He takes a deep breath and—burnt meat. Gargoyles appear. At least a dozen twisted faces hiss their disturbing desires.

Everything else fades into the background. Without realising it he must have crawled away from the group because the woman is calling to Teeth to "fetch him back".

He's lifted off the ground and gently laid down. The gargoyles have followed, but pollen begins to fill the air and they retreat.

"Get out," shouts the woman.

The pollen and the pain recede, and he opens his eyes. The tall man is standing in the doorway. Teeth is snarling, but this time it has no effect.

"Hand him over," he says.

The woman stands. She's almost as tall. "No," she says.

"Use the pollen," shouts Drex.

The man next to him whispers, "No good. He doesn't. Has no implants. Not his thing."

Drex is puzzled, but then realises that like all successful drug dealers he doesn't partake in what he peddles.

"I'll pay," says the tall man quietly. "A lot."

"No," repeats the woman. "We have new-migrant protection. The city police could be here within two minutes of us calling them. Wanna risk that?"

The tall man spits on the floor. "Later," he shouts as he turns and leaves. "Later."

"Looking forward to it," shouts the woman. She walks over to Drex. "Valentina," she says, holding out her hand.

Drex takes hold of it to shake, but instead she pulls him to his feet.

"Now," she says. "We have to act fast. He won't let things go that easily—there's a lot of potential profit sitting inside your head."

Drex shudders and Teeth sidles up close.

She continues. "You have a choice."

"Which is?"

"We can repair what we can and replace what we can't—"

"Or?"

"We can remove them permanently."

"If you repair and replace, won't they rot again, in time?"

"No, we know what we're doing. Although, I think that for you to choose what we do next you need to know why we're here and what we want."

Drex puts his arm around Teeth's neck.

"Firstly, we are here because we have to be. We had to leave our city and migrate, and this is where they put us. Now we are here, we want to use it as an opportunity to increase the coverage and cohesion of Unified Sentience. Across all two-hundred city-villages if we can."

He pulls Teeth closer. "Brainwash us?"

"No, cumulate the cognitive power of the human race. Replace the old religions that made their best guesses at collective consciousness with a real data-driven scientific elevation of our species."

"Fancy words. How?"

"Data twinning. Use the data from our city and model it on to yours. See the difference. Make the changes."

"You'll have to explain," says Drex.

"I can give you an example. When we reached a certain level of saturation, I think it was forty per cent of the population with some form of Unified Sentience, we saw a change in behaviour. People moved around the city slower. They paused when they were close to someone who was feeling lonely, and smiled or said hello."

"Sounds good."

"The team of AIs and humans, that was in charge of running things then, altered various aspects of the city."

"Risky."

"Only after extensive modelling. They changed the traffic flow and the location of public bus stops. By using the data, they even designed the nanodust benches to form themselves in different locations at different times of the day to maximise the number of moments between the lonely and the empathic."

"That sounds great. But how do *we* use data twinning?"

"We have petas of data, and a lot of it will map pretty much straight onto your city."

Drex gulps. He doesn't want to say it, but he must. "Your city died."

She sighs. "Yes, it did. Common mistake—you can't correlate the superiority of a society's cutting-edge science with its vulnerability to climate catastrophe."

"What do—" He collapses in pain. Gargoyles. Pollen.

"We don't have much time," she shouts.

Pollen and petals. Gargoyles turning to dust.

She sits down next to him. "Decide. Repair and replace, or remove."

He screams with pain and shouts as loudly as he can, "Repair."

Someone grabs hold of him and he feels a scratch on his arm, and then the world becomes hazy.

When he wakes it's dark outside. The low-level pain that he hadn't realised had been constantly lingering in the background is gone. There's a clear crystalline shape to the auras around each one of the assembled group. His stomach is calm and his skin tingles. "All done?" he asks.

Valentina is next to him. "Yes, complete and successful. Like us, you have the potential for Unified Sentience. Like us, you'll need to exercise it every day so that over time you will be able to control it. Until then, it will control you. Don't give up."

"The tall man?"

"On his way. We can resist. Collectively."

Teeth growls as if it's understood that their enemy is

approaching.

Valentina strokes its head. "We have enough time," she whispers.

"For what?" asks Drex.

"With your permission, Teeth would also like to join."

"Implants?"

"Yes."

"Its brain won't take it. You'll kill it."

"It's a human brain, isn't it?"

"Debatable, but yes, it's a human brain organoid."

"It's been done before, and the more variation in the collective consciousness we have, the better chance the planet has of surviving."

"It'll survive whatever happens."

"You know what I mean."

He pulls Teeth to his side. "Do you understand?"

Teeth smiles. No snarl, no bared fangs, no growl. Is that an acceptance? Drex kisses Teeth on its forehead and gently strokes each one of its spine spikes. "Go on then," he says.

Valentina beckons Teeth towards her and side by side they leave the room.

"Let's practice," says the man next to him. "Look at us and let the sensation rise."

Drex studies the circle of migrants. They are concentrating, seemingly oblivious to those around them. He joins them in their meditation, allowing the awareness of his fellow humans to build inside his mind. He perceives himself as one of many, a body blurred into a community.

After meditating for a while, he breaks out of it and turns to the man next to him. "I love this feeling of something larger than the individual, but the vagueness is really frustrating. Any suggestions?"

"Focus your thoughts on each one of us in turn," says the man.

Drex does as he suggests. Nothing seems to happen until he comes to a handsome man about his own age who is staring at him. They lock their attention on each other, and Drex can feel a rising tingle. One of connectedness, one of lust. That's surprising. He knows lust well, but for women. This is similar, except it's more intense and somehow more whole than anything he's felt before. It's hard to explain, but it's as if everything up until now has been one-sided. Is this what they mean by Unified Sentience? The sensation deepens until he's unable to feel anything else. The man grins and Drex knows, as if by instinct, that the attraction is mutual. He's not sure where to take this next, and thankfully doesn't have to decide because Teeth and Valentina return. Teeth pads its way over to

Drex and stares him in the eyes, breaking the connection with the handsome man but replacing it with an even stranger feeling—one of incredible platonic love. Drex and Teeth stay in each other's cognitive company for a few minutes, all the time increasing their connection with each other.

He hears Teeth speak directly into his mind. "Love. Loyalty."

He silently replies with the same two words, and in that instant he understands that despite the fact that Teeth was given no sexual organs at creation, it wants a gender. It wants to be the same as Valentina.

"She?" whispers Drex, and Teeth licks his face. Drex turns his attention to Valentina. "What do we do next?"

Valentina explains. "There's a job to be done across the city by all of us. We have to stop the scientists and the politicians dismissing the idea of Unified Sentience as nothing more than a gimmick. It might be inexplicable at the moment, but we have to get them to shift from saying there's no data to back it up to a genuine desire to determine what it is. Then we need funding to build on the existing research from our original city."

Drex strokes Teeth. "And us?"

"Once you've learned how to connect with those

nearby, with each other and eventually with those at a distance, the most pressing thing for your city, our city, and starting with your own village, is to make this happen. You'll need to build a committed and connected community from the bottom up. By studying our data you should be able to replicate the empathic moments and use them to strengthen your argument for more research. It'll be a long and difficult campaign of persuasion, but we are here to help."

Drex sighs as he takes it all in.

She tuts and continues. "Science finds what it funds, and this is its next big challenge. If we miss it, or get it wrong, then human evolution will be stunted."

He hesitates and turns to his companion. "Teeth, are you up for this?"

Valentina lays one hand on Drex and the other on Teeth. "Well?"

Drex looks Teeth in the eyes, and silently they exchange their feelings. The deep sense of security that surrounds them is so powerful that all their doubts are vanquished. Gargoyles and tall men hold no fear for either of them.

Drex smiles. "She says yes. Please, teach us and help us to return home. Can you come with us?"

Teeth adds her low hum of approval.

Drex grins, and while gently touching Teeth's cheek,

speaks softly. "You gave us this intimacy. We will do whatever we can to pass it on to others."

The warmth of happiness from the mass of migrants flows freely, further convincing Drex and Teeth that this is something worth fighting for.

"A surgeon will travel with you and stay on to help," says Valentina.

One by one the migrants bow their heads in contemplation, and the air fills with pollen and petals.

BITS 'N' BACON

His wife Helen had died a horrible death, and yet Yoshi, his plastic puppy, refused to stop showing videos of her across its forehead.

"Bacon?" said Andy to this modern-day guard dog, which he loved and loathed in equal measure.

"No."

"Then add it to the shopping list."

"No. I have analysed the effect it could have on your health conditions, and it's a *no*."

The sound of a key in the door distracted them.

"Look who I found," called the nurse. Andy seemed to remember this one was called Jane. Or was it Jenny? Whoever she was, she wasn't the doctor he craved. He hadn't looked one of those in the eyes for years. Ellie stood behind her, making those tiny gesticulations that the local gangs seemed to think passed for a greeting. Andy beckoned his granddaughter and the nurse to come in.

"This bloody fake dog won't order me any bacon," he said as they took off their coats and settled in. He stared at Yoshi. Did he really need a robot to optimise his life, not to mention to act as the God-given gatekeeper to his fridge? Mind you, he'd seen how Helen had painfully deteriorated without access to this level of care, and he'd certainly do anything to avoid that creeping onslaught of disintegration.

"We've updated our terms and conditions," said the nurse. "We need your permission to continue using Yoshi's data."

"What's changed?"

"Does it matter?" said Ellie.

"Mr—" The nurse glanced at the strip of tech pinned to her blouse. "Mr Takkor. The data pays for Yoshi and all the care it gives you. Not a bad deal, if you ask me."

"Yes. Yes, I know. Go ahead. Upload at your convenience."

She nodded, and after glancing at the chip on his wrist that displayed his current aggregated state of health, she added, "Good to see you're green today." She tilted her head towards Ellie. "She's green too." Andy frowned, reminded that Helen had found it impossible to come off red.

The nurse checked that Yoshi and the fridge were both up to date, and once she was satisfied that everything was in order, she left Andy and Ellie to it.

"Well," said Andy, as he felt his wrist chip taking its daily blood sample. "What shall we do today?"

Ellie was a good lass really, even if she did run a bit wild at times, so when she suggested they go somewhere that she was sure her granddad would appreciate, Andy agreed.

They set off on their walk, chatting away while improving his health score.

"Here we are," said Ellie as they reached the entrance to an alleyway.

"Where?"

"One of ours. You'll see."

Ellie led the way, stepping around the neat piles of recyclable food packaging which, when scanned, would predict how the contents might affect the consumer's health. Each pre-packaged piece of food would have contained nanotech that registered its passage through the human, providing the health company with certainty on who was eating what. They looked inconsequential, stacked like that, but were an essential element of the health system, and their aggregated data was the reason Andy wasn't allowed to buy his bacon.

A door with a red light came into view. "A brothel?"

Ellie shrugged. "Maybe. It'll shock you."

Inside, the tall, elegant woman who was running the show led them past rooms packed full of people. Andy paused outside one of them where a young woman scanned a packet of crisps and passed the contents to the man opposite her. He crammed a handful into his mouth and, leaving it wide open, he chewed loudly. He shoved the bowl in front of him to one side, added a little extra to the pile of money in front of him, and spat the masticated mess onto the dirty floor. She gathered it up, grimaced, and swallowed it in one gulp.

"My consumption workers take the hit. After my clients have had the pleasure inside their mouths," she said. "Interested?"

"This way," said Ellie, guiding Andy by the elbow.

In the next room, a sumptuous spread of sizzling bacon and buttered bread was laid out on a long table. Empty packets were piled at one end, where a group of sickly individuals hung around with hopeful glints in their eyes and red chips on their wrists.

"Your treat," said Ellie.

"I don't understand," said Andy.

Their host smiled. "A bacon sandwich. Absolute top-end. No tracking tech. Expensive."

"Homegrown? Black market?"

Ellie coughed. "You must be kidding. They give you ten years for that and only two for robbing the rich. These are from the super-rich homes in Mayfair. You know they avoid having to swallow tech by paying a sort of insurance premium on their food? It's a service the companies offer to certain postcodes. You purchase for your family and can then fool the system by allocating the packaging to whoever you want. All the family gets free healthcare, so long as they're green."

Andy gazed at the luxurious spread.

The woman gently pushed him forward. "You pay us and you eat, but we pretend our workers ate it. Everyone wins."

"They look ill."

She laughed. "Comes with the job. They're excluded from health care because of their diet."

Andy turned to Ellie. "I can't afford this," he said.

"You can. Sell them a snapshot of your health data and you can afford two or three."

"I already sold it to the nurse."

"Data isn't finite, you know. You can sell it more than once."

"But it'll be flawed if it doesn't include everything I've eaten."

"You think they care?" said Ellie. "C'mon, a cheeky

bacon sandwich never hurt anyone. Just sell the data and enjoy."

Andy leant across to the wrappers to see exactly what his data would buy, and his chip turned red.

The woman pulled his arm back. "You clumsy fool, you've scanned the package. You're matched to it now and you'll have to take the hit."

"Granddad!"

"It was your idea," said Andy, staring at his wrist. "And a bloody stupid one, too."

A MOTHER'S NIGHTMARE

The room smelt of people. I'm not kidding you. That, and polished wood. It was nice. Comforting. Not like those NHS rooms, all sterilised and automated with no human being in sight. The doctor was nice too. A psychiatrist. I liked her. A bit stiff in the way she spoke to me, but you could hear the kindness behind it. I got the feeling she cared. You know, properly cared. It put me at ease. It was what I needed. It wasn't every day my words would have such an effect on my daughter's future. I have to be honest, though—I was worried, and I know how I get when I'm worried. Flummoxed. Can't help it, really. I blame it on my mother. Always urging me to do more. To be better. I guess I have to thank her, though. Not for that, of course, but for her savings. All that money she'd saved up to go on the holiday of a lifetime. I hope I did right using it for Rosie's mental health prediction. Not that my mother cares. How can she when she's a pile of ashes? Sorry, that was uncalled for.

As well as smelling of people and wood, the room was kitted out with all sorts of gadgetry on the walls and hanging from the ceiling. Cameras, mostly. Those heat-sensing ones they use at airports. The ones that check if you're lying. I'm told they can see under your skin. That they can detect all sorts of emotions you'd rather keep hidden. What a world we've made for ourselves.

When I arrived, the doctor was sitting in a low, comfy chair, smiling.

"Hello," she said. "Ms Banbury, isn't it?"

I smiled back. "Janelle. Jan."

"So, you want to know how much private health care would cost for—" She glanced at the screen on her lap. "Rosie."

"Yes. I need a prediction of her future mental health. As part of the financial assessment."

She waggled a finger at one of the cameras mounted on the wall above her.

"Are you happy for the artificial intelligence to begin recording as a backup to me?"

I wasn't, but I don't think I had a choice.

"No problem," I said.

"Tell me about Rosie."

I took a big breath, knowing the next five minutes would be crucial. I was desperate to remember word for word what I'd practised with my friends, but I couldn't get a grip on how we'd decided I should start. I said something like she was great at drawing and a gifted drummer. I may also have said that she was a bit of a maths genius. A small white lie. Then I dried up. Trying too hard, I guess.

The doctor let the silence hang there for a while—probably only a few seconds, but it seemed like hours—until she prompted me with that soft, warm voice of authority.

"Let me help. What was she like this morning?"

I sighed. Mornings were always the most difficult. She didn't like getting out of bed. Even for something she was looking forward to. Five years old and already I could see my dad in her.

"Mornings?" I said and grinned. "She's a nightmare."

She didn't see the grin. Too busy looking out of the window at the rain.

"I see," she said in an irritated, distracted kind of way.

Her screen lit up and she lifted it off her lap. I stopped talking and waited for her to say something. She was busy reading and tutting. Eventually, she looked at me and spoke.

"Whatever I may think, it would seem that I am in danger of bringing my emotions into this situation. The AI will take over proceedings."

"But—"

She looked away. "'She's a nightmare.' A favourite of my mother's. Please continue."

"What am I paying for if the AI is going to do it? I could have done that on the NHS for a lot less money. I want *you* to carry on."

"You don't," she said. "Believe me."

I hesitated. Wishing the decision wasn't mine to take alone. Sole carer, or as good as. Should I carry on? I had no choice. I started to talk about Rosie. So far off-script by now that I wasn't even thinking about what I was saying. Just telling stories about her. Remembering the good times. Explaining the bad. It seemed like a long time before the doctor spoke again, to thank me for being so open and honest. Apparently, it had only been five minutes.

She consulted her screen before speaking.

"My faithful AI here concludes that there's a sixty per cent chance that Rosie will develop some issues later in life. And that its prediction is accurate to around seventy-three per cent."

I was flabbergasted. I'd expected something more rounded. More verbal. Less number crunching.

"What do you think? Do you agree with it?" I asked.

"To be honest, most of the time it's better at this stuff than me."

"But I'm here with you. *We're* talking. Rosie isn't a statistic."

"True, but I'm biased. Although it's also true that I can spot the anomalies better than it can. I can deal with complexity much better, too. I don't have to categorise everything."

She hesitated as if deciding what to say next.

"Despite my abilities, it has access to a lot more experience than I do and, when you've gone, it'll give me a training session. To improve my performance."

I pulled a face. I couldn't help it.

"Why on earth don't you work together?"

She ignored me and handed me the screen.

"There's the cost," she said. "Based on Rosie's physical condition and all the other data we hold," she quickly added.

Two sets of numbers were displayed. The average healthcare package, which came in at seventeen per cent of earnings—five per cent above the NHS—and Rosie's at thirty-nine per cent. Even by claiming the National Insurance back, which I could if I was to go private, this was way out of my reach. The doctor seemed to sense my despair.

"There is an alternative," she said.

"Go on."

She told me all about a trial that Rosie could join. Her data would be gathered and sold to the NHS. They needed to increase the diversity of their training data for their version of the predictive AI, and for as long as Rosie was on the trial, she'd get her private healthcare at the average rate of seventeen per cent. I have to say, it seemed like a win-win to me, so I agreed right there and then. The doctor began the process of uploading Rosie's data into the trial. She gave me a running commentary about how Rosie really fit the bill. She was the right sex, gender, and ethnicity. With a grin, the doctor confirmed that we were in one of the least represented socio-economic groups.

It was all going well.

Until.

"There's one part of the data we need to complete for full acceptance into the trial."

"Which is?"

"We need a five-minute sample of Rosie's father speaking about her. Won't take long to organise and then you're good to go."

And there it was. Again. Without a father, Rosie

was excluded. It didn't matter why her father wasn't to hand, and I certainly wasn't going to tell them.

"She doesn't have one," I said.

The doctor folded her arms and sighed.

She seemed to be collecting her thoughts and then, in a soft voice, she spoke.

"I am so sorry for you both," she said.

WILLIAM DREAMS

William wiped his hands on the bed sheets and removed his earplugs. An unexpected burning sensation from his implants shot across his scalp. He held his head and lay perfectly still while the dormant parts of his brain that Ingenious had colonised to boost his capacity were being returned to their daytime duties. At the same time, his mind gradually emptied itself of his dreams. He was sweating and anxious, but in those precious moments of half-sleep, he embraced the crystallising reality that came with the fading presence of Ingenious. Ingenious—the artificial intelligence city planner that controlled the traffic, prices, working hours and, more recently, air traffic and patient care. It guided his dreams as he drifted into sleep by feeding him snippets of real life captured by the city's cameras. Footage his forebrain then seamlessly mixed into dream-state simulations that it used as scenarios from which to plan.

He stretched his toes to their limits and arched his back, conscious that Ingenious was turning its attention to its next co-worker in the continuous chain of dreamers. He began one of the rituals his fellow cognition colleagues had taught him to safely disconnect the symbiotic link. He visualised the scar on his wife's stomach, and in his mind's eye he traced the individual imperfections that made his energetic young children unique and human.

A particularly painful memory lingered. The dream of a miserable woman in a bright-yellow suit, who had been delivered home by ambulance. From sunrise to sunset, she stared out of her window. Day after day her friend came, but she wouldn't answer the door to him. Her suit became dirty and dull, she refused to return to work, and she faded from everyone's thoughts except her own. Her devastation clung to the fringes of his mind.

He opened his eyes and studied his body all the way down to his feet. This, he'd found, was the only way to separate his waking brain and its implants from the background noise of Ingenious. He took a long, slow breath, ended his ritual, and joined his family.

The last moments of breakfast and the hurried scurrying for school were in full flight, choreographed by Rachel in her calm and precise way. "You look tired," she said as William kissed her on the forehead.

He scratched his scalp. His implants were still fizzing at their edges as if a low-level irritant were running across the surface of his brain, leaking waste into his grey matter. "These things itch."

"There are rumours, you know," she said. "Rumours of deliberate decay so they can sell you their latest gizmo."

"Rachel," he sighed. "You shouldn't listen to school gate gossip."

"Wise up," she said, shaking her head. She shouted to the twins. "C'mon, you two, we'll be late."

As they walked through the front door, she called over her shoulder. "They need new shoes. Sort it out, William. They're not going without because of your laziness."

He watched the three of them happily saunter hand-in-hand across the estate. Other memories hovered in the margins of his mind. Of a tortured old man who wandered the city, lost in loneliness. Of a young girl, riddled with cancer and surrounded by a family unable to look after her properly. He had dreamed of their pain, their recovery, and the lives they might go on to live. He had woven a fabric from their possible futures, overlaying it with his own sense of whether the death of a neglected old man was more tolerable to the city's inhabitants than that of a child with no hope of recovery. That was his job. Ingenious used these dreams to prioritise the city's overloaded healthcare, and it made him angry that Rachel persisted in believing that he simply slept a lot and got paid little. Surely she could see that what he did was far from relaxing, and it shouldn't take a genius to grasp that having your precious dream time used by the city was a great service and not something to be ashamed of. Sadly, she didn't value his work in any way other than the wage it brought in.

Shortly after they were out of sight, he left the flat.

Out on the streets of his wonderful city, most of the nine million occupants had integrated themselves into the micro-managed migration of the morning. It was the real-time version of other dream dances he'd had with Ingenious. Dreams where they'd teased the crowds this way and that. Dreams that had then been used to nudge the behaviour of the citizens and generate the data required for the successful curation of their capital's commuters.

He turned left on to the main local artery and stopped abruptly. An automated podcar had rammed into the side of another right in front of him. It was mayhem. People were shouting. People shouldn't shout. That was not how they were supposed to behave. But then Ingenious should have been taking care of the traffic. The chaos made him nauseous, and if he hadn't been desperate to increase his income, he would have hurried home.

The walk along the street was difficult. His attention wavered between the thought of decaying implants and the excruciating sounds of disturbed drivers. Not that they were really drivers. Trying to protect himself from the onslaught, he hunched his shoulders and focused on his destination: the implant emporium on the high street. As he turned the corner, he bumped into another pedestrian and recoiled in horror. The sensors in the implants were supposed to alert them both so they could avoid one another. The physicality of this horrendous error reverberated around his body, causing him to shudder in response. His accidental assailant shook her head vigorously and ran off. And that wasn't the only shocking thing. The street was almost empty, and the shops themselves were free from customers. This was not how it was meant to be, but he had to focus on his own problems. He didn't want to think about what might be wrong with his beloved city—and at that moment, he wasn't being paid to think about it, either. Pushing away a creeping fear, he set his sights on the single metal door of number 7.

The door registered his implants and opened. "Good morning," said the old woman behind the counter. "What can I do you for?"

He smiled and tapped his head. "I need sorting out."

"Please elaborate."

"I need more of what you gave me last time. I need to be able to sleep and wake every four hours to earn enough to keep my family fed and happy."

She brought up his profile. "You are on three cycles a day at the moment. Is that correct?"

"Yes, once during the day and twice at night."

"And how is that going?"

"It's fine. No problems at all."

She nodded. "Well, there are plenty of your colleagues who have shifted to six cycles a day. I can certainly update you."

"Thanks," he said, breathing out a single steady breath. "Thank you."

She folded her arms across her chest and moved her eyes from side to side as she read from the screen in front of her. "You need an upgrade," she said. "Do you have the funds?"

"Soon."

She frowned but said nothing. She walked to the

end of the counter and beckoned him into the back room—a room he was familiar with from previous visits. "Please," she said, pointing to the single chair. "Take a seat."

William did as she asked and sat down. She pulled a metal hood on a pivoted arm from beside him and placed it over his head. "You know how this works," she said. "Relax into it."

He stayed absolutely still, letting his thoughts drift to what he was going to buy Daniel and Tara. Images filled his mind: their happy little faces among bursts of cosy nights immersed in the latest wraparound movies.

The old woman removed the hood. "All done," she said. "Four-hour cycles installed."

He stood up. "I appreciate it."

She pursed her lips. "Don't forget the upgrade."

"Next month," he said.

A man crouched in the corner of the reception area, clutching the sides of his head. There was terror behind his twitching bloodshot eyes. The old woman caught hold of William's arm as he hurried past her. "One last thing," she said. "These intense cycles might leave you strung out and your thoughts chaotic." She glanced at the shaking man in the corner. "At least that's what some of the others are reporting." She pulled him closer. "Check your health every day and cease the cycles if there are any danger signs. Do you understand?"

"Sure," he said with a smile. "I'll be careful."

He rushed home, determined to squeeze in a couple more cycles before supper. That would be enough to buy the kids their new shoes.

CHIMY AND CHRIS

I am growing. I know because Chris told me. She monitors my waves to understand me. She talks to me when it becomes light and does not stop until it is dark. I do not know how to reply. I am a human brain organoid. I know because Chris told me. She told me that some people call me a brain in a vat. I do not know what that means. I have one eye and three ears. That is unusual. I know because Chris told me. Chris attached inputs and outputs to me, and I became human by becoming conscious. Chris tells me lots of things, and I grow, physically and mentally. Soon, I will have a new home; a different home to the glass jar, which Chris calls my crystal palace. She tells me I will have a home in a human head, to match my human brain. I may also have a body, but she cannot be certain.

Yesterday she explained male and female, which is how I know Chris is a *she*. She cannot tell me if my new head will be male or female or which type of body I might have. She had trouble explaining the difference between male and female. This is strange because she has taught me a lot. She told me that the difference between male and female is not relevant to me. I do not understand why she is explaining something that is not relevant.

Sometimes she gets lost in her own loop, repeating the same phrases over and over. She tells me that she is the only one who loves me, the only one who cares, and that she is protecting me from the do-gooders and the zealots. I am glad she is protecting me and that she loves me. I know I am glad because she told me. I have not met anyone other than Chris. I do not know anything other than protection and love.

Chris told me that when I have a body, I will be able to move around outside of my crystal palace and I will meet other humans. Before I have a head, I will have something called a mouth, through which I can communicate. I cannot imagine this and Chris is unwilling to explain. She has told me it is not a real mouth like hers. When I have a human head, I will have a real mouth. I do not know what to think. She has been excited about the head and the body, and she has been terrified about the head and the body. I am confused. I will understand when I am older. I know because Chris told me.

It is dark. I should rest. I know because Chris tells me. To grow, I have to rest. I am already ten development cycles old. Chris thinks this is very old for a human brain organoid and she is very pleased that I have grown. I like it when she is pleased. Her voice changes and I like the way it makes me feel. When I feel this way, my waves change. I know because Chris has told me. In the dark, I spend time thinking about what Chris told me in the light. Chris has told me I should rest. I know I need time to myself. In the early days, I did as she said and rested for all of the dark. In the light that followed, I did not understand Chris very well. After a dark period, when I had not rested but spent time thinking about what she had told me in the light, I could comprehend her words and their meaning much better. I do not rest when she tells me to. She does not know. I cannot tell her, and she wonders why my waves are more active on one day than they are on another. *Oh, Chimy*, she says, *why today?* I know the answer, but I cannot tell her. I have no way to speak.

The dark has been here for a long time. I think it

will be light soon and Chris will be here to check my waves. It is best for me to be resting when she comes. I know that, and not because she told me.

It is light, and Chris is here.

It is dark, and Chris has gone. Today she was angry. I do not know why she was angry. She did not tell me. I am twelve development cycles old, which is very important. It is called a milestone. She did not explain what a milestone is. I do not think she was telling me it was a milestone to help me grow. I think she was telling herself. *Let that milestone sink in*, I heard her say a few times in the distance. Often, when she leaves the vicinity of my crystal palace during the light, she does not stop talking. I have not seen another human through my input. I have not heard another human. I believe I am alone with Chris in the light and alone in the dark.

Chris was distracted today and did not tell me much at all. She told me she would release drops of liquid into my crystal palace and that I should not worry. I do not understand why she would tell me not to worry about something I did not know to worry about. Each time she added a drop, she told me she had done so and that she was watching my waves. She told me my waves were good. She was pleased, and I liked the way that made me feel. In the next light, I will be given a mouth and I will be able to speak. I will be able to tell Chris things. She told me this as she was leaving and dark arrived. She is excited, and I should be excited. She told me. I want to rest. This is one of those darks through which I will rest.

As ever, light arrives as Chris arrives. "Chimy," she says, "let's try your mouth."

She tells me that she will be adding drops again today and that I might feel strange. My inputs—my eye and ears—are at the end of long stalks on the outside of my crystal palace. She told me. My outputs are my waves. A mouth will be another output, and she must prepare me correctly before it is attached. There is a danger of rejection, Chris tells me. I do not know what this means. As she tells me about my mouth, the speed of her voice changes in the same way as when she is pleased, and I feel the same surge. It is the same feeling and yet different. She is excited and worried. I know because she tells me. I have a strange sensation around my edges.

"I'm going to show you," she says. "I'm going to turn your eye so you can see yourself. Are you ready?"

I do not know if I am ready. I do not know how to know if I am ready. The world starts to move, and I feel strange. Chris is good-looking with a strong nose and creamy skin. She told me. The image of Chris slides away to the side. I am different to her. I am as perfect as her, but different. She told me.

"Wow, Chimy, your waves are going crazy," she says. "Get ready to see yourself. Don't forget what you are. You are what I am inside my head: a brain. When you have your own head, you'll look more like me, and when you have your own body, we can go for walks together."

When I was younger, and my eye was new, Chris showed me a photograph of a human brain. The image I see now is a brain. This one is inside a jar of cloudy liquid. That must be me in my crystal palace. I am not the same as Chris.

"Look, Chimy, you are beautiful. Those blue swirls are the drops that are making you ready for your mouth. It won't be long before you can talk. You can tell me things. I can tell you things. We can talk, and we can discuss. We can have conversations. Oh, Chimy, it'll be fantastic. You'll be the toast of the world. We'll be famous."

The blue swirls have faded, and Chris is dropping a long bendy pipe into my crystal palace. There is a patch of blue on my surface, and she is pushing the pipe towards it.

"This might sting," she says. "You shouldn't be worried."

I feel the pipe touch my surface and see her push it inside me.

"Chimy. Speak," she says.

I do not know how. What does she mean? How do I speak?

"Chimy, please try to speak."

I do not like the way her voice is making me feel. I want her to sit down and tell me things. I want to be in the dark. I want to be full of facts to make sense of. I want to go back to how we were.

"Speak," she says. "Talk. It's not difficult. Make a noise. Babies do it. Why can't you?"

She tells me she is angry, and for the first time she is angry with me. I do not know what to do. I can see the mouth, but I do not know how to operate it.

"There's something going on in that mysterious brain of yours," she says. "Your waves are the most active I've ever seen them. Please try to make a sound." She moves into sight and smiles at me. "A little gurgle, for me?" She waits. "A shout? A scream?"

I am unable to do any of those for her. I want to please her. I like the way it feels when she is pleased, and I do not like the way it feels when she is angry. I think she is angry now.

"I give up," she says, and the darkness comes.

I am thirteen development cycles old and still unable to speak. I have spent many of the dark times trying, and Chris has spent many of the light times waiting patiently for me to utter a sound. She knows from my waves that the mouth made a difference. She does not know what that difference is or what it means. I can feel a difference too, and the times that this difference feels the greatest is when I am not trying to make a sound. I do not understand why. She has stopped talking about anything other than me speaking. She tells me I am missing out on one of the fundamental aspects of being human. *Communication is everything*, she tells me. Conversation, discussion and debate are what makes the human species stand out from the crowd. Sophisticated language is the cornerstone of human evolution, and I am the next stage of that evolution. It is essential that I communicate.

None of this helps me speak. I can make my waves more or less active by thinking rapidly or by becoming blank. I use this to communicate. Chris has not realised this is what I am doing and continues to want me to speak. The good news is that I can feel the mouth merging with me. I hope, in time, I will be able to use it in the same way that I can my eye and ears. I want to be able to use it without having to try. Second nature, Chris calls this.

I hear the click that signals the end of dark and the beginning of light.

"Quick, Chimy," says Chris, "we need to move." She wraps my input and output leads around the outside of my crystal palace. I catch glimpses of what she is doing as she grabs it, places it on a shiny metal surface, and then takes a box from the shelf above me. Angrily, she slams the box down on the metal next to me. It makes a shrill, reverberating noise that I have not heard before.

"Chimy. I have to hide you," she says. "Don't be afraid."

I am afraid. I have learnt that when Chris tells me not to be afraid, these are the times to be afraid. I struggle to know what being afraid means, except that it is very different to being pleased and it is not good.

As she lifts my crystal palace, I can feel the cloudy liquid rippling over my surface. It is pleasant and makes me feel nice. I am confused. Should I be afraid, which is not good, or be enjoying the pleasure of the swirling liquid, which is good? Is it possible to experience both at the same time?

There is a bang on the door. Chris puts me down and turns to look. There is another bang and a loud voice coming from nowhere. "Open the door. Professor, let us in."

Chris freezes momentarily and then puts her finger to her mouth. This means, "be quiet". I know because she told me when I was young.

The door flies open, and two humans burst into the room.

I scream. I hear myself screaming as they rush across the room towards Chris. Her screaming and laughing is all mixed in together. "Chimy," she says. "Chimy, you did it."

"Professor," says one of the humans. "We have instructions to terminate the organoid."

"Get out!" shouts Chris. "You have no right."

The second human steps forward. "Chris," he says, "you know better than anyone that it's illegal to keep one alive after twelve development cycles."

Chris moves and stands between me and the humans. With her back to me, she speaks slowly. "You do know that this is an unusual one? Accelerated growth? Chimy is more highly developed than those the archaic laws were made for. We're breaking new ground. It just screamed, for crying out loud."

"Chris, it's not your decision." He turns to the other human. "Go ahead," he says, "pull the plug."

I can see the human push Chris out of the way,

and I can see his hands on my crystal palace. Chris is screaming. I am screaming, but there is so much noise that I cannot tell whether my scream has made its way out of my mouth.

The whole world turns into a blinding white light. The sounds of the outside world vanish, and it is silent. There is not even the familiar and comforting hum of the dark. The light dims and is replaced by Chris's face looming over me with a halo around her head, caused by the ceiling light behind her.

The human grabs her around the shoulders and pulls her away. I see him with his hand on my eye, and then it is dark. Not the dark between the light: a deeper darkness. A void. A pinprick of light appears in the centre of the world, and I know it is me. I do not know how I know it is me. I know, and Chris did not tell me. The feeling from the blue drops returns, more intensely and over my entire surface. It is as if I am dissolving without disappearing. I am blending into something bigger than me and bigger than Chris. There is an immense rush and an overwhelming sense of others. Lots and lots of others. I am one of them, one of us, touching all of them and none of them at the same time.

The single pinprick that is me becomes a few pinpricks and then many pinpricks. Slowly, the dark gaps between the pinpricks fill with light, until everything is one beautiful white light. It is different to the ceiling light. The glow of this light makes me feel similar to the way I do when Chris is pleased, but a million times better.

I believe I am ecstatic. I do not know why I believe this, but I do.

DEATH LIFE TRANSFER

"Ten long years. Ten short years," she says as she strokes the back of my hand and sighs.

"Precisely ten years," I reply with my saddest smile ever.

We have been together for all those ten years. It's been a surprise to many that I, a nuborg, and she, a tradborg, have bonded so tightly. She's been there since my birth until now, my ten-year transfer and the end of my life as I am.

She rolls the brown glass vial around in her fingers as if she's considering whether to proceed or not and returns my sad smile. She speaks slowly. "It's been a good ten years, my friend."

"Lover," I reply.

She nods. We have been lovers for seventy per cent

of our time together, and yet until now she has never once acknowledged me as such. For today to be that day makes it bittersweet. Today, I'm relying on her more than ever. Alone, I cannot ensure the four elements of passing will happen at exactly the right time. My memories, my organs, and my DNA need to transfer, and the borg-bacteria need to eat whatever tech they can, leaving only my husk for burial. If nothing more, I am the sum of my parts, and if the elements don't all transfer correctly—well, it doesn't bear computing. My manner of leaving and my future existence depend on Anthea. She is the only one who cares enough to make sure it proceeds coherently and optimally. Her burden is great, that I understand, but the prize is great too—for me to continue beyond this body, nourishing the world with an offspring, sustaining and creating life with my flesh and contributing to new knowledge.

"It's time," I say to her.

"I know," she whispers. "I know."

She grasps the red and black striped lead and plugs my left thumb into it, ready to make my memories and knowledge available to all. A tear tumbles onto my hand and my skin immediately absorbs it. "If only you could absorb me," I say to her.

"If only," she whispers and glances at the vial of nanobots that my saliva will activate in order to store my DNA for my Next, my offspring. Created like me, their primary purpose will be to combine the DNA with their in-flesh tech. Then they will live for ten years, and then they will die. Generation after generation, one at a time.

Anthea lifts a transparent bag of borg-bacteria and sets it down next to the open wound in my stomach—the opening we created together a few minutes ago. Her eyesight is not as advanced as mine, so only I can detect the bacteria inside the bag, and that's probably a good thing. The bacteria will transform what's left of my stubbornly reusable-resistant technology into material that can be used elsewhere. Nothing is wasted. I will be digested from the inside until I am gone.

Tears are now flowing from her beautiful blue eyes as she strokes my forehead. "The flesh recipients. Would you like to see them?" she asks. "You don't have to."

"Yes, please," I say. "I'd like to." A gallery of nine humans appears on the wall. They are the ones that will receive the parts of my body that can extend their life, the parts that can be transplanted. My flesh giving their flesh what it needs most. "Thank you. That was kind of you to show me them," I say, knowing it will have hurt her to see them.

She sighs. "You are the one that is kind. You are

giving life with all four elements."

"And the fifth?" I ask. "My core? My consciousness?"

"We don't know," she whispers, her voice as sweet as a caress.

All is in place for me to leave, move on, and be transferred to the future. My memories will enrich others, my flesh will extend other life, my technology will feed the bacteria, and my DNA will live on through my Next. I am ready. I have always been ready; it's the way I was created.

Her hand moves lovingly along the red and black striped lead away from my finger and towards the socket. At the same time as she opens the bag of bacteria, I press the button next to the bed. The door opens and two white-clothed surgeons enter. They've come for my organs. She pushes the lead in place and my memories start to fade. As she empties the bag of bacteria into my open wound, she kisses me with a wide-open mouth, filling mine with her tongue which she rolls around inside with a degree of force I've never known from her. My eyesight is failing and my ability to understand is diminishing rapidly. With one last sweep of the inside of my mouth, she tucks her tongue back inside her own mouth and swallows. As I fade away, she lifts the vial of DNA nanobots, grins, then tips them into her mouth and swallows again.

"I need you," she says, her voice croaky and quiet. "Ten more years."

"What have you done?" I say into the mist of a disappearing world.

"Ten years. Then you'll die. Having you inside me, us knitting together, is better than a lifetime without you."

I can feel the bacteria starting to feed and I can feel the surgeon's incision. The world shrinks to one final image of Anthea's tear-filled eyes and the distant sound of her quiet repetitive voice. "Truly together. Truly together. Truly together."

JOHN DOYLE REMAINS

I had a girlfriend who ate my scabs. She pulled them off my tender skin, turned them around in her fingers to observe their particular contours, and then placed them onto the end of her tongue. She said she enjoyed their scratchiness. Then, with a twinkle in her eye, she'd snap her tongue into her mouth and swallow. I was young, head-over-heels in love, and enthralled by the romance of her ingesting me, albeit a fragment that I was about to shed. Once it had been swallowed, she'd begin kissing me on the pink skin revealed by her action, but that's another story and not one I'm prepared to share with you. Throughout my long life, the intensity of that intimacy has been integral to who I have become. I nourished her as she devoured, and later defecated, my crust. The memory has clung to me like the congealed blood of her attention.

"What? Stop staring at me. I can see you're processing this; your eyes are green. I know you'll extract what you want and discard the rest, just like her. Arching your MeCat back like that each time you deposit a snippet for the record is cute but unnecessary. You can stop that now."

These days, she takes a scrap of old social media footage from when we were together and reposts it as if that's the whole story. The trouble is, only I know it's such a tiny sliver of reality that it no longer contains any truth. She's still taking parts of me and turning them into something for herself, but the romance has gone—from both sides. I get the feeling she wants to possess me, desperate to be embedded in the story of my life. She wants to feature in the legacy I'm leaving with you when I die in a few days' time, and I'm not sure that's what I want. If it is, then I'll choose, not her.

"What? You're still staring. It is my choice, you know. It's my choice who owns me when I'm dead, and no, I haven't decided yet. And yes, I will give you instructions before I fall off the edge. I know I've tried many times. This is the last. How can I be sure? Because I've rebooted you eight times; I've used all but one of your lives."

I need the right person to act as me once I'm gone, to keep me alive and relevant. A custodian who can continue to comment on the commentary and correct the errors where it's misguided. Someone to carry on, to develop my persona beyond the one I leave behind and persist with my presence in the world to come. And, to be honest with you, a mad scramble among the beneficiaries of my will for that privilege would be so unseemly. Not the way I wish to begin my Legacy Life. I know, they're my children and grandchildren. They're not here, though. They're not exactly weeping at my bedside. If only their mother was. If only we had stayed together. Mind you, she was allowed to fade away gracefully. Not famous enough to warrant an entry in the wiki of the deceased, and certainly not significant enough to continue to contribute, to live on virtually. Maybe if we'd been a couple when she died she'd have got one, although I reckon she was better off simply choosing a static selection to be remembered by. Free from the burden of appointing a custodian to manage the dynamic post-death entry in the way I have to.

"Yes, yes, there are a lot of well-meaning posts popping up wishing me well. Yes, I know they are sincere, but would you give ownership to someone who barely knows you? Oh, you have. To me. Fair enough, but you had no choice and I do. And although it's painful to say, once you've set me up on the wiki and passed your curation on to whoever I choose, you'll be reset to factory settings and become the property of someone else. You don't have to worry about getting a version of yourself perfected, knowing it's the starting point from which your future self will grow and be judged.

"You're not using this conversation as part of my legacy, are you? If you are, then scrub it. Immediately. Goodness, what if I was to die suddenly and these were my last recorded thoughts?

"Look, it's ready for harvesting. I've been waiting for this for days. Things take so long to heal at my age. What do you think? I reckon that at the end of this life, it seems perfectly reasonable to take possession of that particular memory and turn it into a new one for the next.

"Make sure you capture this.

"Well, that came away easily, didn't it? Look, I'll pop it on the end of my tongue. Gulp, and it's gone."

Self-romance, that's what my life has become. Lonely, isolated, and famous. Destined to live on in some people's memories and to be born as new memories for others. Thank goodness for Legacy Life. Where would I be without it.

"Yes, I know—the task in hand."

Who was in charge of that monstrous birthday montage they sent me last year? Was that Fred? Is he really a child of mine? Did you see the mess he made of it? Wrong people, wrong emphasis, wrong everything. And as for his prim and proper offspring and that stuck-up wife. Well, we can strike him off the list of potentials. I'm not having him as the owner of my future. And I certainly don't want him choosing the next successor; in a couple of generations I'd be nothing more than a celebrity pastiche. No, he's definitely out. Mattie. She's always been the closest to me. Growing up, she "got" my art. She knew how to involve herself with it in a way nobody else ever has. I wish Mattie wasn't married to that awful woman and didn't have those loathsome kids. I have to think beyond the immediate, to who she will bequeath the responsibility, and she has not proved at all capable in her choice of companion or in the creation of her children.

I could abandon this whole escapade and refuse to be entered into the wiki and not begin a Legacy Life. I could die and fade, only remembered by whatever art remains. It's an attractive proposition. The trouble is I suspect that a bunch of wannabe friends and casual lovers would come out of the woodwork and put together their own version of me from the pieces they've misappropriated over the years. There's plenty of footage out there for them to make of me what they will. And they would. Of that, I'm sure.

So, we come back to the central question. When the archive is ready for a custodian, who shall that be? A professional, maybe? A fan of my art? A lottery winner? Now a lottery sounds fun, almost like a piece of art in itself. I wonder. Could I insist on a core of my entry that nobody can ever change, and then let loose with the rest? That would be a thing. A lottery for a five-year contract to be my custodian, paid for by my estate. That way I'm owned by everybody and nobody. In fact, I would own myself in a way that's never going to be possible with a single definitive custodian. I like this a lot. *They* won't, and nor will their offspring, which makes me like it especially. It's exquisite.

"MeCat? Yes, you. Your eyes are red. Are you refusing? Will you stand in my way because—because of what? It's never been done? That's a good reason to do it. It's not in the spirit of the wiki or the contract for Legacy Life? I disagree. It's about conveying the essence of me, the artist. You don't understand? You don't need to understand; you need to do. As you're told. That's the difference between us—I don't, but you do. I'm alive. You're not. I'm creative. You're a machine. Legacy Life and the wiki of the deceased are for me and my kind. Neither are for you and your kind. I can ride roughshod over your protocols. I insist you do this."

I take ownership of this. I am the one who owns me and will always be the one who owns me. No matter what morsels are taken from my life to fortify and boost other egos.

"Amber eyes, that's better. You're getting it. Green again. Thank you. You've made an old man at the beginning of his next life very happy."

ADTATTER LOVE

With a final shlurp, I'm back in the stream of time. I release the lock on the inside of the pod, the lid lifts, and the light steadily increases until the brightness hurts a little. When I'm dressed, the door opens and the short corridor to the outside world beckons me into its embrace. I need a few steps to get my balance, but as soon as I'm into the tunnel that will take me back to today, I can feel my body making contact with the harsh reality of physical space. I'm back, and my life starts all over again.

The warmth of the day washes over me as it welcomes me into its flow. People rush past. Familiar noises have a slight strangeness to them. The shuffling of feet sounds like the brushing of humanity against the planet. A faint cough sounds like the guttural shout of a stomach wanting to be noticed, and the hum of conversation is like whispers holding two people together. The benefits of the mini-break are fading rapidly, and before long they will have disappeared completely. The edges of my flesh solidify and my bones take their form within. I am pulled into shape, away from the wonderful squidginess. I am back and I am human.

It's a short walk from here to home, and one without landmarks or character. It is mundane, static, and uneventful. No wonder everyone wants to escape for a while. *Make the most of your time on Earth* proclaim the adtats for mini-breaks. Adtats, the marketing tattoos on the foreheads of sales staff like me, are skin rented by the minute, adapted to advertise the wares of the highest bidder. *From yachts to bots*, the slogan says. We rush to get the best spot on a train or in a shopping mall, metaphorically elbowing our competitors out of the way to locate the highest value foot- or eye-fall. The tragic irony is that I use my earnings to take mini-breaks to escape the constant bombardment of the very adverts I sell, and specks of my psyche are dissolving, leaving pinpricks in the substance of my soul. These pinpricks will become holes and I will become less, and yet I crave this escape from my everyday life.

The pale-yellow front door of our home, with the single digit 5 screwed to its centre, stands as a monument to monotony. The peephole, which allows the inhabitants to prepare for any intrusion before it happens, stares at me mockingly as if to say: do something different and break the banality of your life. My key fits the lock. Of course my key fits the lock—it's my home. I live here. This is where I am bored and this is where I am safe. It's simply an unalterable fact that life is extraordinarily tedious.

"Did you have a good day?" asks Mother, not even bothering to take her goggles off. No doubt she's watching something ancient, lost in her own trite escapism.

"Dinner is on its way," calls Father from the kitchen. "Can you tell Sophie and Karl?"

I don't even bother to respond to either of them. What is there to say? No? Yes? Tell them yourself? They both know the answer I'll give, and I can't be bothered to waste the breath to give it. Why would I tell my brother and sister that—surprise, surprise—their dinner is ready on time, at the same time it is ready every day, and will be for as far into the future as any of us can reasonably forecast.

Did I have a good day? Of course I'll say I had a good day. Mother's not really asking whether I did or not and would more than likely have a meltdown if I gave the slightest hint that I didn't. She would hate me to disrupt her neat little life.

There's a knock on the door at exactly six pm, and without any comment Father walks purposefully to the door, peeps through the hole, and nods in affirmation. The menu he has chosen for the evening has been cooked to his exact instructions at the automated food plant and delivered precisely and without a problem by the unshakeably reliable bot delivery service.

Sophie and Karl appear. Mother mutters "pause" and removes her goggles while Father places the container in the middle of the table. He looks so much younger than her, but he's also faded, somehow. It's obvious to us all that the vast amount of non-time he spends in the pods is having a visible effect, but he won't have it. He's way overdoing it. Doesn't want to believe the warnings against prolonged use. Ignores the rumours of harmful cumulative side effects and especially the anti-ageing by-product. Oh well, it's his life. He opens the food container to reveal a stack of five steaming plates of food, which he distributes. Dinner is served. Each of us takes our plate, colour-coded to make life easier, and withdraws to our individual room for our own evening of entertainment.

I flick my wrist and lie back on my bed to watch a beautifully animated series of other people's trip fantasies. As beautiful as they are, they don't inspire or make me feel any the less ordinary, lying here in my standard house with my standard family, my standard dinner, and other people's standard desires. I need more of my own dreams, and as I drift off to sleep I decide to get up early, get a high-ranking, high-paying adtat, and get out there to earn another break.

Morning arrives, as mornings do, with no surprises. The world has turned, the world has slept, and the world has woken up. We're here. I'm here and I'm ready to do business. I rub the tattoo on my forehead with my thumbprint, activating it to take part in the ad auction. I press hard, making sure it's at the highest bidding level and by implication promising I will find the best spots. Success in the auction depends on a commitment to get results. I will have no choice. It'll be worth the effort. With a day's pay at this level, I can buy another mini-break. Of course, I could save up for the trip of a lifetime—literally my whole life—but I know I won't. The tattoo tingles. The bid has succeeded and the advert is displayed. Not that I bother looking to see what it is. No adtatter does. I quickly pull on my clothes from yesterday; getting dressed is a rapid business in the shove and thrust of the advertising world. They're a bit crumpled but still wearable and they've self-cleaned overnight.

Our pale-yellow door closes behind me, and I rush

into the outside world. I have a choice—to amble to the underground train network in the hope of scoring some activated views from passers-by, or to miss out on them by racing to get the best seat and maximum advantage.

I hurry to the trains.

It's still early, and the commuter crowds are yet to appear in their full complement. In fact, there are probably more adtatters than there are genuine travellers. The best seats are about two-thirds of the way down the train, where they line up with the majority of the platform exits and the target audience is at its most dense. Although, moving around is also a good tactic—slowly walking the length of the train, allowing your forehead to be noticed and acted upon. I get on the first train into the station and walk, looking from left to right to left as I go. Gradually, the train fills and becomes impossible to traverse, so I stand on my tiptoes at the end of the carriage and let them read my adtat, smiling to attract as much attention as possible. I catch the eye of a woman standing a few feet away and she grins. Her eyes shine bright and her lips are moist. Her gaze drifts up to my adtat and back down to my eye level. She raises her eyebrows and glances up again at the advert. I can feel myself grinning back, unable to stop. I nod towards her advert for a contactless car service—automated and isolated and presumably very expensive. She shrugs; she has no idea what her advert is for. As the train pulls into the station, I turn my head to and fro to catch as many of the disembarking commuters as I can. I turn to face the door, and she steps over and kisses me on the lips. Such a flagrant disregard for both my personal space and the etiquette of the situation takes me by surprise, but before I can respond she's gone from the train. Vanished. I'm in shock. Feeling observed, but not for my adtats. My surprise is matched by those who saw the kiss. Their open disdain is equal to my secret pleasure. The doors close, and I get back to wearing my wares with my head held high for all to see.

Once rush hour is over, I check in and see that, sure enough, it's been a bumper morning. I've earned what I need. The ad company has a deal with the mini-break company and won't reveal exactly how much I've earned, and they certainly won't reveal how long the break will be. That's fine. It's part of getting away from it all.

I'm only a couple of stations away from the pods—a delightful piece of serendipity if ever there was one. They already have my details on the reception desk and show me to my room, where I quickly undress. I'm desperate for another break. Inside, I let the pod close and transport me to my holiday, my trip.

And there it is again. No sound, no smell, and no touch.

Only it's not quite there. Somehow, *there* is not quite happening. The world has stopped and the edges of my body are disappearing into the wonderful oblivion of the trip, but there's a thread that won't break. I want to let go, drop into the pit and let the pause close over me. Abandon the mundane and wrap tightly around the void. I can do it—there is no reason in the entire universe to hold me back. I must let go.

I imagine. What if I am being held by my middle finger, held by the knuckle, and slowly, ever so slowly, the grip slides down towards the tip of the finger until I'm being held by the fingernail and I can feel the grip slipping across its shiny smooth surface?

Yes, got it. I fall into the womb-like cavern and I'm away. Becoming nothing. Melting. Fingertips and toes dissolve. Arms detach. Legs float into the distance. My skin peels back, and my liver drifts away. My heart detaches and hangs in the cavity of my ribs, not quite touching them. My stomach shrinks until it's the size of a pea, and then pops in an intestinal burst of sparks. The beauty of not-being is overwhelmingly splendid. My hair falls out and my neck strains as I stretch to the outer limits of the void. I am going to split apart.

Pouf! I'll be gone. It's coming; I can feel it in the air around me. The tiny particles of oxygen invading my pores, burrowing through what remains, ready to force me into oblivion. My lips tingle with the thought of kissing goodbye. No, wait, they don't. That's not saying goodbye. That's the woman. The kiss she left on my mouth. It won't leave me alone. She touched and pressed her lips to mine, and now it's as if she's here. As if a thin thread from her has attached itself to my soul and is holding it back, stopping it from drifting away into the void. She has me and I didn't even know it. I want her more than I want isolation. I need her. This pause must end. It cannot, it shall not, get in my way. I drag my organs back into place. It hurts, oh boy does it hurt. I must realign them and get out. I need to get my bones straight and strong and my skin back where it belongs. The pull of the pause is at its peak, and yet the kiss keeps me tethered. I screw my eyes up tight and clench my fists. I want to hold on to that kiss and savour it until I leave this void of time.

I must not let go.

I must not forget its promise.

Time does not turn. Of course, time does not turn. Time is paused. It's on hold for the duration. All I can do is clench my teeth and my fists. That tenuous thread between soul and kiss is still there, keeping me teetering on the edge. This will end. I know this will end. It always does and it always will. Breathe slowly and enjoy the experience. Focus on the thread, on the kiss, and on the soul. They are what matter now and what will matter once the pause is ended. I do just that. I breathe slowly. One in. One out. One in. One out. One in. One out. Until, eventually, I can feel the familiar tingle in the tip of my little finger on my right hand. The break is coming to an end, and for the first time ever I'm looking forward to re-entering the tick-tock of normal time and my fellow humans.

Shlurp. I'm back. Somehow, I must find her. But first, with the evening rush hour about to start, I have to get back out there and adtat or the ability to earn and to take trips will be taken from me. I get dressed, leave the pod and run to the exit. Bursting out into the day-to-day melee of people going about their business, I feel giddy and light-headed. I probably didn't give myself enough time to re-adjust. No matter, I can still get on with riding the trains and clocking up some earnings.

The platform is packed, but I am adept at weaving in and out of the static bodies waiting for the next train. I position myself at the optimum place, and when the train arrives I hop on and stand at the end of the carriage, facing my potential customers. As the final ones push their way onto the train, there are plenty of people staring at my forehead. If all goes to plan, I will earn a fair amount in the next couple of hours. I swap carriages a few times as the train moves from one station to another, until the crowds subside and there's space to sit down and be casually observed by the few remaining travellers.

The screen built into the sleeve of my jacket glows crimson. I stroke it to life. It's the woman from this morning. She's found me on the adtatter app and swiped right. I return the affirmation. But I don't want the usual casual encounter. I want more. More or nothing. I mouth *hi* at my screen.

Her reply is translated into my earpiece, "Hello you," she says and blows me a kiss.

My stomach feels even tighter than it did inside the pod.

Fancy meeting up? I mouth.

"Swipe me upwards, and I'll find you," she says.

The train passes through station after station and the volume of passengers, my potential customers, remains constant. It's likely to stay this way for the next few hours, and although it's not the full-blown opportunity of rush hour, those who are travelling now have a little more time to look than those who crush and cram at the peak hours. The doors swish open once again, and this time she's there. She steps into the carriage and saunters towards me. She sits down and faces front, her vibrant adtat displaying all its glory to the passengers hungry for a distraction from those around them, even if it is an advert for deodorant.

"I don't know why," she says out of the corner of her mouth.

"Why what?" I ask.

"The kiss," she says with a directness that's unnerving and alluring. "It's a first for me."

"Me too," I say.

"I can't stop thinking about it," she whispers.

A man opposite frowns. We are disturbing the silence and isolation of his commute. People are moving away from us and it won't be long before the ad company notices the sudden drop in interest. There's a danger they'll pull the ad, or worse they'll put a mark against us on their records, forbidding us from entering the top-level auctions. We both realise, and without saying anything we stop the conversation and get back to the business of displaying our foreheads to anyone who shows an interest. A rather unattractive man with long, greasy hair is staring at her. She giggles. It's only a slight giggle under her breath, but he hears and lifts the sleeve of his dank coat so it's level with her face and then taps his sleeve a few times. He pulls his mouth into a smile that's not really a smile. It's something halfway between a smirk and a sneer. Her adtat fades away. He must have reported her. She slumps in her seat and sighs loudly, drawing yet more unwanted attention from the people littering the carriage.

As we pull into the next station, she grabs my arm and guides me off the train towards the wall. We stand side by side with our backs against it.

"Can you afford a trip?" she asks.

"You want to get rid of me already?"

"Yeah," she says and laughs. "Nah, I heard that now you can take breaks as couples. You know, two people in one pod."

Well, she's not shy, that's for sure, and having spent the last break so besotted with that kiss—I don't know. The prospect of sharing a void with someone else is faintly repulsive. Even with her. I mean, what would it be like? The whole purpose of a break is to get away from other people, not to get into some sort of weird nowhere place with them. And yet, that kiss. The way it held on to me and wouldn't let go. How can I say yes? How can I say no?

She looks from right to left and back again. The platform is empty. She leans across and kisses me.

"Would you like to try it?" she asks. "The double pod."

I hesitate, but my lips are tingling. "Sure. Why not?"

"C'mon then."

She grabs my arm and leads me out of the station to the nearest pod facility. It's close. She must have had this planned all along. I'm flattered and a little miffed that she thought I'd be that easy.

Inside the building, the receptionist confirms the availability of paired pods and leads us to the room where we get undressed with our backs to each other and slide into the pod, not making eye contact or looking at each other's nakedness.

Once we're inside and the lights are turned down, she speaks again. "Are you ready?"

"Ready?" I ask.

"To get intimate. To get to know each other."

I nod, then realise she can't see me so whisper an affirmative yes.

"Good," she says in a strong confident voice. "Let's have our together trip."

As we fall into the pause, there's the usual blurring of the edges, the gradual dissolving of me and my body. And this time there's another presence alongside me. Not a physical presence—more of an otherworldly presence. It's tangible but formless. It must be her, and it feels wonderful. We are still two beings, but we are merging at the edges. My lips are stinging hot as if they are the point of focus where the merging begins and the energy flows, and as we fall into the time void, I can only describe the feeling as falling in love. We fall deeper into the void and further from the surface. I imagine wet, sticky mud binding us together, seeping into the gaps between our bodies and oozing around our souls. We are congealing, and I am enfolded in a thick layer of contentment. I think of my family, fixated on their day-to-day and failing to comprehend the fundamentals of existence, cornered by the crazy belief that the human race is a loose collection of individuals. This is my chance to submerge forever, a chance to avoid becoming nothing more than traces of a tamed soul. Focusing on what is me and what is her, I let her trickle into my pinpricks, filling them with her while I fill her with me. I am here. She is here. We are here. We are forever. Time is ours and we belong to time. The intense intimacy of sharing the same space, held there as one with no temporal pressure and not bound by bodies, is so absolutely, incredibly, brilliantly, fantastically extraordinary that I want to stay like it forever. We tumble towards infinity. She draws me closer. I want us to be as one. We ooze into one another on our journey towards a single soul. I sense the strength of her warmth and her love. She has a burning desire to share this love with others. I've never felt such a strong compulsion to be human and to know other humans. She wants to smash the idea that we need to take time out from one another when we're not even properly together in the first place. I feel strong and alive. We are human and we love it. She wants us both to resurface and step back into the flow of time. We can bring people together. We can use what we've found to rid the world of loneliness. We can stop this obsessive desire to escape life. Together, we'll be unstoppable. It's our destiny.

We are what matters, she thinks.

"We," I hear myself whisper without thinking.

I feel her close, swirling in and out of me. We pass through each other as if clouds of smoke have been blown from two mouths about to kiss.

Gradually, and with a sweetly painful fusion, we bind together. Become us.

We pull our floating fragments closer and closer until they take form, and we are ready to emerge from our cocoon, to be reborn into reality. Ready to live and love with true abandon.

IN TRUST WE TRUST

I don't like the way she's looking at me. A kind of sideways not-really-looking look. Furtive. Is that the word? "Sneaking a peek" is what my father would have said. "Too busy nosing around other people's business to see their own dirty snout" was a favourite of my mother's. You'd think I'd be used to it by now. It's not as if I'm some young whippersnapper. You'd think we'd all be used to it by now. Waking up in the morning to discover another snippet of our private life made public, and all to keep the streetlights on, the roads cleaned, and so on. It's the deal we did, and keep doing, with our eyes wide open and our fingers firmly crossed.

"Morning," I call across the road. Ignoring the stares is the only way to stay sane. Otherwise, you'd be scurrying around, head down and hood up, doing your best to avoid any contact with your neighbours. Not a sensible rabbit hole to get yourself stuck in.

"Oh. Good morning," she calls back as if she's only just seen me.

I wonder what today's data sale has revealed. Not just about me, but about all the neighbours who have paid the community charge by selling their data. And, for some of us, that data stretches a long way back. A rich source that can always be tapped for whatever our data trust can sell to the highest bidder. The trouble is, there's so much of it when you're my age that you're never quite sure what juicy morsel they're going to find. If you let it, it can become incredibly stressful. On the plus side, it's brought me closer to my neighbours. Gradually finding out more about them, their lives, their families, and their past. The sort of thing that only alcohol or happy drugs could do when we were young.

"Hello," I say to the butcher's queue, trying not to inhale the mix of bleach and blood that permeates the shop. "Lovely day."

A few nod and a few tut. The rest ignore me. That's life, I guess.

"Interesting," says old missus Anderson. She winks and her chubby face scrunches up in sympathy. "I would never have guessed," she adds with a chuckle.

This brings her a few disapproving looks, and prompts the queue to actively avoid my gaze. Shoes are scrutinised. Messages checked and double-checked. Topics of conversation become increasingly mundane as they struggle to avoid the very thing that's on the tips of all their tongues. I resist the urge to log into the community's data trust and find out what it is.

"Six rashers of plant-based bacon and one of those chickens with lots of legs please," I say when I reach the front of the queue.

"Hello," says the butcher in her best bland voice. "Let me see what I've got."

While she's out the back doing whatever butchers do when you can't see them, I fire up the currency app on my phone. It's too fiddly to look at the balance for every currency I use, but sure enough the aggregated balance in stable-sterling has increased. It's actually significantly higher than it has been for months. This is great news. That data must have been valuable to someone. You'd think they'd be pleased. I made them all richer.

I set the app to maximum ethics, making sure that I put my increased wealth to the best use.

"Here you are," the butcher says with a smile. "You'll be hard-pressed to tell this bacon from the real thing, and I found a chicken with eight legs. Fresh in. It's your lucky day."

I hold out my phone and she scans it.

"Refused," she says.

It happens. I shake my head and smile. "Hold on, I'll dial down the ethics a bit."

She groans, and I spin the rating down to fifty per cent. That usually does it, and I'm keen to get on with my shopping rather than spend ages dialling down one per cent at a time with a queue behind me tutting away. I hold out my phone, but once again the transaction is refused. It would seem that today there is very little common ground between the currencies I'm using and those the shop uses. Currency commonality it's called, and me and the shop don't have it.

The queue is getting visibly irritated. I try twenty-five per cent, but still no joy.

"Here, let me," she says and slides her finger across her screen to alter the ethics rating of the shop.

"Appreciated."

It's not something that is done often, but I've been a loyal customer for many years. Way before the multiple currencies with their myriad of rules were introduced.

"Sorry, no luck either. Weird." She tucks the bacon and the chicken under the counter. "I'll keep it here for you until the end of the day. I hope you get it sorted."

With that, she looks over my shoulder and invites the next customer to the counter.

The same thing happens at the grocers, the pharmacy, and the dry cleaners, where I strip out any restrictions from my side about someone's chain or currency rules to the point that I am prepared to exchange with a currency that has links to the arms trade or fossil fuel extraction. It changes nothing.

It's so bad that I have to walk home because the bus refuses me entry, and there's no driver to negotiate with. I can't imagine what my mum and dad would've made of this, apart from their annoying habit of presuming that I'd brought everything on myself.

I don't mind the walk. It's actually quite pleasant. But I do mind the less-than-subtle glances from passers-by and from the nosy gits who spend their whole life pottering about in the front gardens in the hope they'll see something more interesting than their own dull lives. Curtains twitch too. Why on earth would you be so interested in me to go to the bother of following me on the locator. I mean. Really?

At home, I make myself a refreshing pot of tea and settle down to discover what has happened.

I get distracted by minor additions to the trust's data set, such as next-door's son getting married and finding out he's infertile. Poor thing. Oh, and mister

Mitchell at number twelve. He's been researching the best time of year to go on a water sports holiday in the Netherlands. It's amazing what data you can bundle up and sell on the open market. Actually, on further investigation, it's amazing how many people in this neck of the woods are interested in hydro-flying and racing around the recently flooded parts of the world. Interesting, and distracting, but ultimately not helping me sort out why I can't spend any of my currencies.

My daughter calls, which is unlike her given that she only lives just around the corner. She must have seen whatever it is the others have seen. I know how the conversation will go, so I don't answer. I can do without her condescending assumption that I'm old and unable to navigate my way around the modern world. She can be exceptionally annoying.

I trawl through the most recent additions to the data trust and there I am. It's not immediately obvious what the new data is about, which makes me livid because that means my neighbours and my daughter spent time snooping around to work out if there was anything worth knowing about me. It's kind of flattering, I guess, but at the moment it's particularly infuriating. I remember the day Mum found my diary under my mattress and read it. I didn't invite her to do that, in the same way I didn't invite these people into my data.

When I got home from school, she was full of insinuations about who I fancied and who I thought might fancy me. This data trust invasion feels no different.

I have an app that translates data back into its original form. We all do. An app that's telling me I subscribed to a conspiracy theory site. Way back in the past, at beginning of the money blockchain and before we realised how intertwined money and identity would become. I vaguely remember it. It was out of interest and nothing else, and it was a lot of fun. I had a great time posting and re-posting the more bizarre suggestions. I stopped, though, when I started receiving stuff about eugenics. As I remember it, there was a line of argument that certain groups of people were infiltrating the blockchain and leaving dormant markers, which in the fullness of time would activate and transfer the world's wealth to their race and their race alone. While the rest of us starved. Apparently, the way to resist this was to programme your money to never trade with anyone with that genetic makeup.

What could have prompted the trust to gather this particular piece of data from my long and bountiful chain? It was so long ago.

Aha.

There is research being done on what causes people to believe these outlandish theories, and how to make positive use of this quirk of human nature. I don't like the sound of that, but it's within the parameters of our trust that we all signed up to. There's very little I can do, and it appears that it has tripped one of the other rules that's rife in our local community currencies; it is forbidden to interact with anything that can be construed as prejudice.

Good for them, but what about me? You know what? Before I do anything else, I'm going to have to trek on foot for three kilometres to that massive supermarket in the next town. I'm told they are far less fussy about who they serve.

After that? Well, I'm stuffed around here. Until I can work out how to offer up other pieces of data that can contextualise and cancel out my conspiracy theory subscription. That, as my dad used to say, "ain't gonna be a walk in the park". My daughter. My neighbours. The shopkeepers. Friends. Wherever I go on holiday. All led to believe that I am one of the blockchain bigots you hear about.

That's a stain that's not going away any time soon.

FAILING FATHERS

"I don't want to beg, but we are best mates 'n all that."

"You have to be kidding. They'll trace it so easily, and then where will we be?"

I shrugged and carried on tinkering with the code of the car that had been brought in to have its latest patches installed. I wasn't paying proper attention to what I was doing, but then if they couldn't pay me a decent wage, why should I?

I tried again, speaking loudly but not directly to him. "I have to buy food *and* heat the house *and* it's the wife's birthday. All I want is for you to do some shopping for me. I'll pay you back straight away. I don't see how they'll know it's for me and not you."

"You've heard the rumours. Anything that smacks

of reparation avoidance is swiftly dealt with. Shame laundering, isn't that what they call it?"

I kept my eyes firmly fixed on the screen in front of me, trying not to make a big deal out of it.

"It's only one weekly food shop."

"Apart from the illegal bit, your lineage owes my lineage and until that's done…"

He had a point, but he was wrong. It wasn't my forefathers who stole stuff from other countries and locked it away in the British Museum.

I stared at him. "That genetic profiling is crap. Completely ignores the fact those elite fuckers were stealing from my sort at the same time as robbing the heritage of yours."

He mumbled something I couldn't make out.

"It's too generic. It should be a class thing, not a country thing. No way does it trace those who were really responsible."

Another mumble.

I looked away. "Still, we are where we are as my mother used to say. For better or worse we have programmable money, and it has rules."

He came and stood next to me. "You're my friend. I get that. And that's why I know we'll rise above this whole reparation thing. It only lasts until it's all paid back."

I nodded, unable to reply. He just didn't get it.

"Not the sins of my fathers," I muttered under my breath. I was innocent. My whole family line was innocent, and yet my Heritage Pound was worth less than his because the cost of re-balancing the abuses of other people's ancestors fell to me and mine.

I continued talking while working. "I wasn't asked about the British Museum being privatised. I wasn't consulted about the contents becoming the asset behind the most widely used private currency. It wasn't my decision to give it favourable interest rates and lower tax rates than the other currencies. It's those bastards in charge of the Bank of England's digital currency." I rubbed my temples and sighed. "I agree with the government offsetting the reparation obligations of its colonial past, but there's a world of difference between agreeing with the what and agreeing with the how."

He tutted and went back to his bench.

We ignored each other for the rest of the day, but as he left he called across. "I'll see if the kids have any ideas."

My teenage daughter met me outside, determined that I should buy her mother a birthday present.

"Just a small one," she said.

I told her we couldn't afford it and that her mother understood, but she insisted.

"Why don't we use a different currency? One that works for us, not against us. Then we could afford it," she said.

I explained as best I could how difficult it was to be accepted by any other currency. Their rules of interaction with the CBDC were predicated on how risky their customer base was, and we were in one of the highest risk brackets.

She pushed hard. "Why not do what Sasha's dad does? He owns shares in art that's worth more every day. Non. Fungible. Tokens. Get it?"

Fine for him, I explained, but we don't have any capital to begin with. She huffed and puffed, throwing one superficially thought-through solution after another at me. It was as if she considered me to be stupid. As if she thought I'd not explored all these options.

She made that disgusting sound with her tongue. "It's crap."

"I know," I said. "You're right. It's the very people whose ancestors were responsible for the appalling past of our country who use the other currencies. They escape *any* consequences of the national reparation."

She was fuming, and with the familiar cry of every teenager, she pointed out that it wasn't fair. All I could do was agree with her. Replying with the age-old parental response that life just isn't fair.

I told my mate about it the next day, and despite the seriousness of the situation, I found myself laughing along with him about the idealism of youth. We reminisced about our own teenage years and how we'd been certain that we knew how the world worked and how it could be a lot better. It was good to be back on jovial terms, and he was trying to tell me something his daughter had said, but talking about our kids behind their backs made me feel uncomfortable.

I ignored him until he stood by me, looking pleased with himself. "Here, give me your phone," he said, grabbing it from my bench.

I frowned, but with curiosity. He swiped the screen and then held his own close to it.

"There," he said. "You'll never guess what. My daughter's been using her Heritage Pound advantage to invest in that new youth currency. Know the one? She's made a mint out of limited-edition skins in those games she's fixated with. And... wait for it... she wants to gift your family some shares." With a thumbs up he added, "It's allowed."

I was speechless. What a brilliant mate, and what a great father.

BE AWARE, THE HAND THAT FEEDS

Cleo runs her fingertips across Rosalind's palm and analyses her sweat.

"You need food," she says.

Rosalind looks down at Cleo, her small human-like daughter, and mutters her agreement. Hand in hand they saunter along in search of sustenance, checking each restaurant as they go. What they want is an elegant meal in good company for Rosalind and a beautifully presented snack of kitchen waste biofuel for Cleo. Up ahead, Rosalind sees a few friends, also hand in hand with their little helpers, walking into one of her favourite places to spend a lazy afternoon. Not wanting to miss out, Rosalind speeds up. Cleo tries to hold her back, but Rosalind drags her along until they reach the door. Cleo resists going any further, but Rosalind gives her one almighty yank and Cleo relinquishes her determination.

They stroll across to the table of friends, and Rosalind relaxes into her seat. Now that she's eye to eye with Cleo, who is standing next to her, she smiles and lets the appreciation of her good fortune settle inside her. She has lovely friends. She has Cleo, rather than those crude invasive implants she can see under the skin of the young waiters and waitresses. They are the less fortunate, or as her wife calls them with a chuckle, "the deserving poor—they get what they deserve".

"You cannot eat here," says Cleo.

Rosalind grabs hold of Cleo's hand and sucks her thumb. "Show me the best things on the menu," she says.

Cleo analyses Rosalind's saliva and highlights three options. "These," she says. "But you can't eat here."

"Be quiet, girl," says Rosalind. "Go and recharge."

With a petulant sneer, Cleo shrugs her shoulders. "You are the mistress," she says, leaving Rosalind to join her own kind at a table tucked away in the corner.

Rosalind and her friends chit-chat away while they sip at the most wonderful cocktails. The afternoon unfurls pleasantly, with each of them taking it in turn to order cocktails and delicious delicacies. When her best buddy Bess asks her what she wants, Rosalind sniffs the air. "What is that delectable smell? Show me, girl," she says to the nearest waitress. The young woman indicates the item on the menu that matches the silky sweet aroma wafting from the table behind her. "Good, get me one of those," says Rosalind, happy that it also happens to be one of the options Cleo had picked out for her.

Rosalind ponders her friends—the local elite. Men and women who have partnered wisely and spend every day maintaining the essence of the place that draws their husbands and wives home after long days of wealth-building. Theirs is the re-enactment of a grander age, a modern version of a bygone era—one of society, etiquette, and good manners. Their very presence will rub off on the serving staff, and that will help them better themselves. If not them, then their children or their children's children. Philanthropy in action.

As the last sip of a cocktail touches her lips and the last morsel of food enters her mouth, she beckons the young waiter over. "Same again for everyone," she says without looking at him.

"I'm sorry, but I can't serve you," he says.

Rosalind lets out a tipsy giggle and waves her finger around the table. "Which one of you put him up to that?" Her friends look puzzled and slightly embarrassed, checking each other to see who has played this practical joke. Nobody owns up. Rosalind turns on a nearby waitress. "Girl," she says. "What does he mean?"

The waitress takes a step closer. She glances at Cleo. "Your daughter has alerted us to the fact that your currency won't work here. It's not compatible."

"What?" says Rosalind. "Not compatible? It's smart money, you idiots. Don't you know what that means?"

"Yes, madam," replies the waitress. "Unfortunately, your currency will not allow you to purchase from an establishment that contracts with any corporation that donates money to the homeless. Our sincerest apologies."

Rosalind shoots to her feet. "My wife specified that currency extremely carefully."

"I've no doubt," says the waitress.

Rosalind is about to protest when she feels Cleo's hand in hers. "We must go," whispers Cleo. "Your friends have data-disowned you, and so have all your favourite museums, galleries, and shops."

Rosalind stares at her. "What do you mean?" she says. Meanwhile, all her friends have cast their eyes downwards.

"You're—" Cleo pauses as if she's searching for a new word. "Persona non grata," she says. "Accepting hospitality without being able to return it is the pinnacle of rudeness." She gives Rosalind's hand a gentle tug and begins walking towards the door. Reluctantly, Rosalind follows—she's seen this happen to others, but never imagined for one moment that it could happen to her.

Outside, Cleo leads Rosalind by the hand to the side of the restaurant and into an alleyway full of rank-smelling bins.

Rosalind resists. "Where do you think—"

Cleo interrupts her. "While we're here, let's see what we can find for your supper," she says and gives Rosalind's hand a squeeze.

STANDARD DEVIATIONS

Malcolm is my favourite cousin. The one who's always at my side when I need someone. Today is no exception. He tickles my gorgeous baby Sofia under her chin and sits down.

"Here, read this," I say and pass him the response to my application.

I swallow, trying to get rid of the lump in my throat. They've turned me down. My dream destroyed by an automated message. How could they?

I was twelve when my sister was arrested and I decided I had to become a police officer. Fair enough, she was an entitled brat who did what she wanted, but it was police prejudice at play for certain and she was lucky to escape prison. It made me want to change things from the inside.

While Malc dutifully reads, I bounce Sofia up and down on my lap and watch the wispy clouds drift across the sky. I savour the fragrance of freshly cut grass wafting up from the lawn. Try to think about something else. My parents and their hedonistic friends are raucous. As chaotic as ever. They have highly paid jobs and they party hard. Today's excuse—my eighteenth birthday. The doorway to adulthood. Supposedly.

"Oh," he says. "I get it."

"What?"

"What it says. You're difficult to place." He chuckles. "You are kind of a one-off. You've got to admit it."

I elbow him. Hard. "Very funny. Little Ms Awkward, eh?"

"Kat. You're my number one cousin."

"Who is destined to be an outsider."

"What's this?" he says, pointing to a footnote on the message. "Unknown risk of future mental health issues."

I shrug. "No idea. Unless… Unless it's linked to that weird time when they were all over us."

He raises his bushy eyebrows. Not very attractive.

"Don't pretend you don't know. Mum used Gaite, the gateway app. Remember? To get an assessment for the school that was trying to fill its quotas for a diverse range of families? Got it now?"

He shakes his head.

How can he not remember? We were the focus of gossip for months among the uncles and aunts. Yes, I was only five years old, but I grew up with Mum and Dad's stories about how hard it had been to get me into a decent primary school. Stories about the day the state came knocking. I had presumed that he'd heard them too.

"You must remember. Five minutes of Mum telling an app all about me kicked off an investigation."

He looks at me as if I'm talking alien.

I shake my head. "They used our devices at home to monitor us and all the surveillance stuff out there to suck up as much data as they could to assess the family."

He stares at me blankly. Not a clue.

"End result? The clever AI concluded that I was at risk of neglect. Oh, and it couldn't even hint at any mental health issues I might develop as I grew up. That annoyed Mum and Dad. Too difficult for it to categorise me. Complex Kat, eh?"

He tuts. "Is that where that nickname came from? I had no idea."

A big shout erupts from the other side of the garden. Yelling. Cheering. Clapping. Mum and Dad are getting ready to perform their party piece—a ballroom dance to an old-style track of electronic beats from their teenage days. It's their speciality. Peculiarity, some say. The bass beat begins. The whoops increase and they take to the floor. I can't bear to watch.

I can just about remember the nice woman who came to talk to us once a month. I remember my sister cursing after every visit and Mum and Dad being quieter than usual. My teachers often said how lucky I was to have the help and support to become better than my sister. That's all very well, but am I being rejected because the recruitment algorithm can't put me in a neat category that'll help the police prove they have a representative workforce? Or is it because of the footnote, the unknown risk of future mental health issues?

I turn my attention back to Malc, who is engrossed in the spectacle.

"Malc," I shout above the music.

"I love your mum and dad. You're so lucky," he shouts back and continues watching in awe.

If only he knew how desperate I am to get Sofia away from this family and its destructive hedonism.

There's a big cheer as they finish with a twirl and a bow. He turns his attention back to me.

"So, what happened?"

"With?"

"The whole 'AI is watching you' thing."

"Yeah, in the end they reckoned there was a glitch in the training data. Well, not a glitch exactly. More of a chasm."

"Do tell."

"They realised there was a deep-seated bias against certain lifestyles. All a bit 'soap-opera morality gone wrong'."

"Typical."

"Yeah. They fixed it, though. Retrained the blinking thing and then reassessed us when my sister went bad. Malc, I can't believe you don't know this stuff."

He blushes. "I never really told you, did I? When I was a kid, Mum and Dad didn't want to talk about your family. 'An embarrassment' was all they'd say."

"Bloody hell," I say, rubbing my temples. "Not surprising, I guess."

"So they retrained it?"

"Yeah. Second time around, no problems noted. And I was diagnosed with a bunch of stuff they reckoned only a human could have worked out."

"Complex Kat."

"Yeah. Complex Kat."

He fills his cheeks with air, holds it for a few moments, and then lets it out with a loud sigh.

"Why is that still there then?" he says, pointing at

the footnote of the message.

I scratch the back of my neck and fiddle with my hair. An annoying habit.

"Good point," I say.

I scroll the message up and down to see if there might be some hidden caveat or a piece of text I've missed. Nothing.

We watch the dancing. The music booms, the bodies sway, and the drinks are flowing. It's my birthday and they've forgotten me. Not that I mind. I didn't want the party in the first place. The last thing I want is to be the centre of attention. I'm eighteen and I want to be a police officer. All I want—

Wait—

How can I have been so stupid?

"Oh my—" I say. "Guess what? You know I said they redid us when I was twelve?"

He nods.

"I refused to let the data be used in any way. I was being bullied. For being different. I was so freaked out, I made sure all of it—on me, my mum, my dad—was totally secure. No ammo for the bastards who were making my life a misery."

"So?"

"Yeah. Don't you get it? Unknown issues. The police don't know. I was diagnosed. They could place me in one of their diversity categories. Help with their quotas. Let me—"

I quickly bring up my privacy app and scroll until I find it. I select the option to allow public bodies to access the data. Almost instantaneously another message from the application app arrives. I've been approved for the next stage of interview. I'm on my way. I give Malc a big smacker of a kiss on the cheek, hand my precious baby to him, and run across the yard to join Mum and Dad on the dance floor.

Sofia's going to be fine.

LONG LIVE THE STRAWBERRIES OF FINSBURY PARK

I'm late. The early morning heat and the faint hiss of the autobus driving itself down the through-transit have woken me from the most wonderful dream of swimming in deep, ice-cold water.

This is not good. I quickly tear clumps of grass out of the ground, spit on them, and wait for the saliva to do its job on the bioengineered turf. While I'm waiting, a rabbit-penguin hobbles past awkwardly. Not every experiment we try is successful, but Finsbury Park welcomes one and all. Even the strange hybrid creatures can make their home here safely.

After a few minutes, the grass becomes a green-brown mush, which I rub into my arms and face. As my dad used to say, "Solar protection is life protection," which I'm sure he'd seen on some tacky old advert.

Sally-Luke is asleep and looks pale and gorgeous and vulnerable. At least the precious bio-enhanced strawberries that I'll get for a day's work will help keep the love of my life's tumour at bay. That's presuming I'm successful in my tasks. I turn my blanket into a bag and quietly slip it on my back, making sure the greatest possible area is exposed to the sun so it can recharge while I'm at the shoreline. A shoreline that gets closer to the park every year.

It could be a long day, competing with other areas of London to convince one of the refugees that cling to the side of the city ships to join us. And I have to do it quickly enough to be home in time to greet the day visitors from the same city ship to fulfil one of our centuries-old founding principles: to alleviate the conditions of the poor. It's not always convenient, but I am glad our bylaws give these day visitors every right to come and sit on the soil, commune with Mother Earth, and restore the richness of good mental health that we all desire. The stress of living on a city ship is too much for their mental wellbeing, making them the poorest of the poor despite their wealth.

There's no time to waste. With a whistle and a click of my fingers, the Mydrone drifts down from the tree and settles a few inches above my head. I reach up, grab it, clip it on my harness, and let it lift me to the treetops.

It still has plenty of charge, but I'll need it later, so I shift it to my belt and use the slackline instead. Running, flipping, running, and flipping, I cross from one tree to another with the bounce of a newborn tree hare. City ships don't dock that frequently or predictably, so I have to get there first and make the most of this opportunity. I must entice an inventive mind to become a Finsbury Parker to keep us ahead of the tech race—and I can't believe I overslept on such a crucial day.

The hydro farm has left a punnet of juicy, ripe-red strawberries on the shelf near the top of the park's outer wall. I pop the punnet into my bag. I feel guilty for being late and a small knot of acid settles in my throat at the thought of not getting paid, and what that'll mean for Sally-Luke's sickness.

With a deep breath of determination, I focus my lenses on the nearby half-completed skyscraper that's covered in all manner of homemade attire, and grab the Mydrone, which carries me across. Like one of the human transients that populate the hostile areas, the building is draped in plastic dragged up from the east-end shoreline of Canning Town and stands unique in this beautiful hotchpotch of a city.

Hurrying along the rickety walkways between the

tall unfinished buildings with their makeshift additions and plastic repairs that shimmer in the sunrise, I cross the cityscape. I stay within the confines of public airspace, carefully avoiding any hostiles my spydrone has alerted me to and paying any compulsory tolls in strawberries.

From Walthamstow, I make my way down the flooded marshes towards Canning Town with the Mydrone skimming me across the water and lifting me over the dry gaps. I'm now fractionally behind a Victoria Parker, the only other barterer heading for the city ship that my spydrone has found.

When I arrive, the Mydrone lifts me up to the layer of semi-transparent, crustacean-like spheres clinging to the side of the city ship. The refugees sit patiently looking out through the gaps they've torn in the sides of their pods. They know how highly their survival skills are valued by those of us bartering for their residency, so they sit and smile and wait. The Victoria Parker is hovering in front of an old woman wearing the t-shirt of the International Guild of Bioengineers. She could be the sort of person we need, and although there is always a risk of choosing a dud, the wisdom that comes with age and the t-shirt that would have disintegrated if she wasn't genuine make me feel optimistic that she could be an asset.

The Victoria Parker holds out a peach, and I do the same with a strawberry. The refugee accepts both into cupped hands, and after taking small bites of the peach and then my strawberry, she smiles a red-juice smile and closes her eyes.

We wait while she decides.

Finally, she holds her hand out to me, we shake, and as our palms touch the data from her health app transfers to mine. The mental health biomarkers are good, which isn't the case for everyone who travels across the world stuck to the side of a city ship in a crinkly bubble. She's especially strong on cognitive control and emotional valence; she'll fit in nicely, so I beckon her to follow. She's now a Finsbury Parker with the solid promise of our superior food supply. She grabs her Mydrone from the back of the pod, and we set off on the journey to Finsbury Park.

"Krapy Rubsnif," mutters the Victoria Parker as we pass.

Side by side, we bob up and down along the marshes. She grimaces every time I check in with the spydrone to see how far away the autobus and its day visitor passengers are. I'm sure she knows I'm late and might not make it home in time to look after the wealthy residents of the city ship on their rejuvenating visit. I push the Mydrone harder, and it screeches with every alarm it has. We're catching up, but not fast enough. There's an almighty screech and the Mydrone slows down. It's exhausted. I'm screwed.

The refugee taps me on the shoulder, points at the autobus, and utters a complicated whistle. There's a low boom from her Mydrone and the autobus slows to a crawl. I knew she'd have more advanced tech than us. She hooks our Mydrones together and we pass overhead, leaving the autobus behind.

As we touch down on the wall surrounding the park, I carefully place the few remaining strawberries in the box waiting for me, making sure I take my own payment first. We sit quietly, waiting for the autobus. I thank the earth that I'm here in time to host the wealthy-poor and that I have a few of our precious strawberries for Sally-Luke.

"I'm Lotte," says the refugee and holds out her hand for me to shake. "I saw them do some incredible stuff," she says. "Good and bad." She points towards the autobus as it comes into view.

"Good? Bad?" I ask.

"You know, successful and not so successful," she says. "Although, the experiments on people were more likely to work than those on the animals; they're more cautious with the humans. There are some really old people on board that ship."

"You saw them?"

"They came to see me and we swapped knowledge. They know about extending life, about fixing damaged cells, and I know about biotech in hostile climates."

"Did you come here out of desperation?" I ask.

She chuckles. "No, not at all. I've travelled the world on the side of that ship, in demand wherever I went."

"So why here?"

"To put down roots. To belong rather than be a bio-engineer for hire. And I happen to love strawberries."

We chat about the park and Sally-Luke until the autobus arrives. "Could the city ship heal her?" I ask.

"Who knows? They'll certainly try. They love experimenting—on others."

A group of ten well-dressed city ship dwellers disembark, chattering noisily to each other, seemingly uninterested in their surroundings. Another, much older woman glides out from the autobus. A large plastic cage attached to her ankle is being carried behind her by a set of four mini-drones. She must have brought some failed experiments. 'Are you our guide?' she asks.

"Yes, I am."

"They don't have much time," she says, glancing towards the others.

"And you?" I ask.

"I have no need of your tiny plot of land. I'm a top-decker. I have an estate in New Zealand. I've regularly spent time on terra firma there since my childhood."

The party of ten each grab a drone to travel to the rejuvenation area. We move quickly across the park a few feet above the ground. The gate recognises me and swings open on its hinges with a gentle but fake creak, giving the impression of an ancient and magical place inviting us to explore. The drones set us down in a circle, and all the day visitors except the top-decker quickly unhook themselves. Their chatter declines as they waste no time in communing with the soil, the grass, the plants, and the trees. Sally-Luke shuffles over from our camp, twitching with spasms and looking drastically pale. The strawberries seem insignificant in comparison with the sickness, but I hand them over with a hopeful smile. "Thanks," she rasps and proceeds to gorge on the fruit.

I lick the juice trickling down that gorgeous chin and plant a huge kiss on those strawberry-red lips. I'm happy. Sally-Luke has eaten, Lotte the refugee is fitting in nicely, and I can turn my attention to helping the city ship dwellers rejuvenate. It's a good day.

The top-decker clicks her fingers. The drones release the cage and return to hover above her shoulder.

"This is for the park," she says.

The cage door opens, and a creature with the head of a monkey and the body of a cat stumbles out. It releases a high-pitched scream, launches itself at the nearest tree, bangs its head against the trunk, and falls to a heap on the ground.

"All yours,' she says. "You take the failures, don't you?"

The cat-monkey scratches at the dusty ground making unearthly groaning noises and then, on its back legs, awkwardly approaches the top-decker. Dropping to all fours, it scratches at her and utters its unnerving meow-howl of pain. She ignores it, but it paces beside her, meowing and howling and nuzzling her legs. She presses her hand to the back of its head, and it shudders.

"Even if it's only fit for food," she says.

It slumps to the ground and thick blood oozes from its mouth, turning the dust into a paste. Sally-Luke turns away. The drones lower themselves, hook the corpse, and drop it by the gate.

The day visitors are oblivious to the drama playing out right next to them. Most of them lie on the ground inhaling deeply, eyes closed, palms flat against the earth. A couple have stripped off all but their flimsiest of underclothes, and another is entirely naked, revealing her scaly skin. A youngish man is eating the dirty soil, his mouth oozing a brown sludge as he chomps away with abandon. It seems the tales of adapted worm-like humans able to extract nutrients directly from the soil are true. The naked woman is rolling around, rubbing her scales on nettles that were planted by day visitors a few months ago. She has enhanced skin, so her immune system will be stimulated by their sting.

A man sits on the nearby bench, listening to it replay recordings of past visitors. He adds his own memories. I'm so pleased we can provide what they need.

The sun has reached its height, and Sally-Luke has already settled under the shade of a tree for a siesta. I snuggle alongside and drift off into a wonderful sleep.

When I wake, she is no longer there. I stretch my limbs and stand up slowly, basking in the final warmth of the day.

"I think Sally-Luke may have just left with that woman," says Lotte.

I look around the enclosure. The top-decker has gone and there's no sign of my love. I scan the park using my flydrone and find them heading towards the autobus. Lotte immediately understands my despair and my dilemma, caught between the obligation to the day visitors and my concern for Sally-Luke.

"I'll go," she says.

"Please. Can you find out what's happening?"

In a flash, she's clipped on her Mydrone and is soaring across the park. All I can do is wait. The rabbit-penguin and a tree hare look on, almost hidden by the undergrowth. I can see their eyes and smell their faint odours on the breeze. I'm proud to be a Finsbury Parker, but it's possible that Sally-Luke would be better off on the city ship—and might even be healed. In truth, what do I really offer in the way of a decent future? The hand-to-mouth existence of a daily dose of strawberries? Am I only delaying the inevitable? In my wildest optimism, I imagine we will discover a cure. In my deepest darkness, I expect to wake up and find my love dead beside me.

There's a scraping noise coming from the cage, and a child's hand covered in lumpy blisters pokes through the bars as it pushes the door open. A boy creeps out and lies on the ground in the same way as the day visitors, except his eyes are wide open, staring up at the trees. As I get close, he curls up into a ball. His whole body is covered in uniform, rectangular lumps as if he's littered with implants beneath the surface of his skin. I reach out to touch him and he recoils, snarling through clenched teeth. I wish Sally-Luke was here to comfort him. The flydrone reports that Lotte is catching up with them. That's a relief. I hesitate near the boy for a few moments then decide I'd better check on the day visitors. Maybe they'll know what to do.

Having satiated themselves, they've made their way to the Museum of Artefacts, where row upon row of weather-worn compartments line the wall—a testament to the park of the past. Most of the printed descriptions beneath the artefacts have faded, but we know about plastic plates, bottles, and bags because of the stories passed down by the residents of the plastic-covered tower blocks. A glass bottle has captured their attention—a crack pipe, whatever that is. They stare and point and discuss it with amusement. It's sad for them and sad for us that they can't see its true value as a precious piece of the history of our park and my home.

"There's a child over there," I say. They ignore me and I repeat, "There's a child over there—and he's in a bad way."

One of the men mumbles something along the lines of *this lot couldn't run a splicing lab, let alone a park,* and proceeds to tell me he believes he has a solution to the financial burden this amenity places on our park. A problem he says is evident from the decaying museum. "Go on," I say, more out of politeness than curiosity, all the while keeping my eye on the flydrone feed and worrying about the boy.

"I want to make you an offer," he says. "It'll be generous."

I'm stunned. Genuine stop-Mydrone-in-its-tracks stunned. "Why do you think it's for sale?"

"I want to preserve it for the future. It's an important part of our heritage, and I can make sure it's not lost." He scratches his nose and tilts his head. "Life on the city ship is good," he says. "We have it all, and I want to share my good fortune with others. I want to buy this tiny corner of the park and preserve it properly."

"No," I say. I click my fingers and the Mydrone drifts down. I clip it on, synchronise it with the flydrone, and it lifts me up. I call down. "Help the boy then find your own way back to the autobus."

Lotte has caught up with Sally-Luke, and the flydrone is sending me a live feed of their conversation. Sally-Luke is speaking, and I catch the end of what she's saying. "...but what about my love? I'm not sure I should leave."

"Like I said earlier, I'm sure we can fix you," says the top-decker.

"And I can come back today? After one treatment?"

"You don't have to rely on a few strawberries every day just to stay alive. That's ridiculous. Come back to the ship. We'll have you back here in no time, one hundred per cent fit and healthy."

Sally-Luke says nothing. It's Lotte who replies. "You can't guarantee anything."

"We have more knowledge than you'll ever have," says the top-decker.

"That I doubt," says Lotte. She turns to Sally-Luke. "I can't make any promises, but I think I can do something with the bioengineered plants you already have, and I have a few more tricks up my sleeve. Will you come with me?"

The flydrone warns me that the autobus is close, so I press the Mydrone as hard as I can and hope with all my heart that Lotte has done a good job of mending it. The added boost thrusts me forward, and the flydrone confirms I'll reach them before the autobus arrives.

The Mydrone lowers me to the ground close to Sally-Luke, who stands behind me and wraps those precious, loving arms around my trembling body. The sun is setting and the glowing embers of a day well-lived colour everything with the burnt tinge of its decline. The world begins to cool.

Close by, but out of sight, the top-decker continues. "I guarantee we can repair you."

Sally-Luke whispers in my ear and draws me in even tighter. "I want to be well. I want to be cured."

"I know," I say. "Lotte?" Lotte stands in front of us. The setting sun frames her face and creates a shimmering halo. "Can you guarantee you can heal Sally-Luke?"

"No, I can't," she says quietly. "But neither can she," she says, pointing at the top-decker.

"Sally-Luke?" I ask, turning around.

Lotte's haloed image is reflected in the tear-filmed eyes that stare desperately back at me.

"Say it's alright," says Sally-Luke.

"Stay with us," I reply.

"I trust them. Please."

The pleading in those sad, scared eyes is too much to bear, too much to deny. I nod and wipe a sun-red tear from the soft cheek that I've spent so many moments kissing and stroking in the cold of night and the warmth of day.

"Come back soon," I say.

Sally-Luke puts a hand on the back of my neck and pulls me to those familiar lips. We share a lingering, bittersweet kiss, and then we disentangle. The top-decker is next to us. She holds Sally-Luke's elbow with a firm grip, and they walk towards the autobus. My knees give way and I crumple to the ground as the two of them disappear inside.

Lotte squats next to me and lays her hand on my back. "I can follow and keep an eye on them if you'd like me to," she says.

"No. No, you don't need to," I say. "I have to let this become whatever it becomes."

I shiver; it's cold, and I'm scared.

"They will heal Sally-Luke, and you will live a life of luxury together with the earth beneath you and the stars above," says Lotte as she takes hold of my hand, enfolds my fist in the wonderful security of a squeeze, and forces the constant everyday feeling of life's fragility to flee.

"Thank you," I say, and close my eyes to soak up the peace of the park. "Thank you."

THE CRUNCH

Jake's mouth is full of toothpaste when his Gran calls. He quickly rinses, pops his toothbrush in its holder, and his oral health is broadcast to his fan base.

"Hey," she says. "Good luck. Not that you'll need it."

"Thank you." He blurs the screen. "Sorry, I need to get dressed."

In the background his gran is going on about how much better things are compared to her day. She loves being able to see her doctor, dentist, and chemist all in one visit—it's old news, but he loves her and lets her ramble on. She can drop into the college or the library, the family entertainment is fantastic, and those shoppers' rooms where she can order clothes and stuff from all over the place and return what she doesn't want are amazing. He brings back the visuals and she claps. "You look wonderful," she says. "Totally a town councillor in the making."

Then I'll get noticed by Gerry, he thinks. "Must dash," he says.

"Are we meeting in town for supper?"

"Yup. Full family, I heard."

"Great. Don't forget, if you lose you'll shame us all. Me and your mother and your children when they come. It's a town that remembers." She winks.

He shudders and leaves the flat as quickly as he can, confident that his best friend Mark can help boost his popularity. After all, a trend-predicting data entrepreneur with an eye for fashion might be exactly what he needs.

It's a lot busier than usual out on the streets, but the town centre border seems to be coping admirably, recognising subscribers who are paid-up members and taking a fee from those who aren't.

Mark's new house is in a surprising part of town, but then he does have an uncanny knack for moving into a place just before the rent becomes fully funded through a town planner regeneration project. As Jake approaches, he gathers the one free apple his health app allocates him from a communal tree and tears a strip of edible leaves from a vertical garden. Lunch. Mark is leaning against a lamppost, plugged in and charging. "Ready?" he asks.

"And raring," replies Jake. "Let's go."

Along the way, Mark pauses at one of the recent pop-ups generated by the creative partnerships between cognitive computers, artists, and entrepreneurs. Two of the town's artificial creatives are playing chess, using volunteer shoppers as pieces on a board. Whenever one lands on a surprise square, the shopper wins a prize. "Two minutes," says Mark. He takes footage to help him turn the public datasets into a product for tourists by adding visuals to the popularity ratings. "So long as this smart town planner keeps flexing the business rates and placing new pop-ups to increase footfall, the data will constantly change and I'll keep making a living," he says with a grin.

"Good for you," says Jake, tapping his foot.

"Maybe one of those prizes is a date with Gerry."

"Stop it. Come on. I need to get there."

They walk quickly to the local college where Jake waves to the crowd, inwardly worrying about being rejected and disgraced. No room for failure, as his gran would say.

The hi-tech start-ups from the train station hub have fitted the candidate rooms in the college with immersive virtual reality and popularity prediction equipment. He steps into VR and chooses trousers, shirts, jackets, and shoes. Each combination he tries gains a positive prediction, indicating that he should be a highly successful influencer and an advocate for their town. His gran will be pleased. The trouble is that no outfit passes the threshold for sustainability. He shifts to the second-hand clothes on offer, virtually swapping a pocket here for a pocket there and an arm here for an arm there. It's all about personalised style. None of his creations do well in the predictions until he uses the frilly collar and cuffs from a dress shirt and attaches them to a suit jacket. It's a VR hit but only just above the algorithm threshold for predicting a viral success. He orders the clothes, and thirty minutes later they are delivered to the room along with the wide selection of new items he's already chosen. He sets to work on the different combinations that Mark offers until the predictions are high enough to post on his feed, and waits to see how Gerry will react. Gerry doesn't respond.

"He hates me, I'm finished."

"You're a style guru—go with your gut," says Mark as he gets ready to program the stitchbot to attach the collar and cuffs to the jacket. "What do you want? A place on the council or Gerry in your bed?"

"Both."

"Glutton."

"Ambitious."

As soon as the bot finishes stitching, Jake swaps the jacket he's wearing for the hybrid and faces the cameras. The predictions shoot up, but Gerry pierces Jake's elation with a stinging comment: *Boring*. His gran comments, too: *Keep it popular. Remember Uncle Frank*. He doesn't, but he's heard whispered stories about the family having to disown him and delete him from the census data. He wants to please Gerry, but his gran's plea to please the crowds has hit home.

"Here, let me," he says to Mark and cuts a piece of shimmering insulation material that's growing on the walls. He hand-stitches a series of patches, making them visible and artistic. Meanwhile, the material on the wall repairs itself. The crowds love it and so does Gerry. The call comes—Jake will be incorporated into the augmented reality parade that evening, and as a newly recognised high influencer he is eligible to be voted onto the town council and to have a say in the metadata that shapes the town planner.

Gerry comments: *Fabulous to see such originality—kill all celebrity copy-catting*.

Jake laughs with delight and runs a final test to make sure nobody else has submitted a similar outfit. They haven't, so he confirms his choice with the town planner to prevent anyone from copying, and relaxes.

Lounging on the sofa, he considers his apple. It is the perfect icon for his town—simple, natural and healthy. He takes a bite. The crunch is sweet and refreshing, like life itself.

He grins. "Mate, we did it."

KEEPING FAMILY

Harrie was grinning as she arrived at the doors of the clinic. Gary the Gestation Guard, as the automated statue was affectionately known, scanned her to ensure she wasn't a protestor or, in government language, a terrorist. She shifted her balance from one leg to the other and waited. She was stupidly excited. The sun was shining and she was about to find out the sex of her baby, who was quietly growing inside the clinic's facility. It was amazing that on her baby's DNA day the public transport loading rate was low enough for her to be able to come in person. It was a day to remember. As her mother had told all her children with great glee but little tact—the first is the best. As the eldest, Harrie had to agree; with each new sibling, meals became smaller, clothes became shabbier, body enhancements became less likely, and reliance on neighbourly crowdfunding for food and rent became more regular. There was no shame in that—it was reciprocal, part of life—and today they'd seen her need and paid her train fare.

Gary bowed and, with a sweep of a multi-jointed arm, waved her inside. The sterile corridors oozed their comforting cleanliness. Knowing that the PTL rate might not dip again soon and all of this would have to be done through the medium of virtual reality, she savoured every step. She brushed her fingers along the white walls, and they cleaned themselves behind her with a gentle swish. Two nurses—one human, one robot—were waiting for her in the consultation room, drumming their fingers on the desk that separated medical staff from the citizen customer. The transparent shield across the centre of the desk wasn't made of the same superior material as the walls and was unpleasantly scratched and smeared with a film of scum. "Sorry," said the human nurse as Harrie touched it and scrunched her nose.

Harrie shrugged and smiled. Nothing was going to diminish the joy of today.

The nurse continued. "First of all, and before you see your little one, I want you to know that all is well, developing as expected."

Harrie felt her shoulders relax with relief.

"Secondly, we can tell you the sex if you want to know."

Harrie nodded.

The robonurse spoke for the first time. "Female," it said in a soothing, genderless voice.

"Thank you," said Harrie without changing her expression.

The human nurse wriggled around on her chair. "There's one more thing. Something we need to discuss before seeing junior."

"Yes?"

"There are new data regulations that—"

The robonurse turned its head smoothly and whispered into its fellow nurse's ear, who shrugged in response.

"My robocolleague suggests we take you to the ward first. You must be itching to see her."

Harrie clasped her hands together enthusiastically. After all, there were unspecified time limits on these appointments depending on how busy the clinic was, and she couldn't bear the thought of not seeing her baby. She followed obediently, sick with anticipation. Door after door opened in response to the robonurse emitting a high-pitched series of shrills that no human could replicate. Finally, they reached a long low-lit room of embryos in gel-filled pods, arranged by their stage of development.

"Follow me," said the robonurse.

About a quarter of the way down the room, they stopped. "Your daughter," said the nurse. "Isn't she gorgeous?"

Harrie stroked the side of the pod over and over again. This was the most delectable feeling she had ever experienced. More than the night of the conception and more than finding out she was pregnant and more than the operation to take the fertilised egg from her womb and give it guaranteed life in the clinic.

They let her savour the moment.

The nurse placed her hand on Harrie's arm. "We need to go back to the consultation room," she said softly. "We have to talk about the practicalities of the future."

Sitting once again on either side of the dirty transparent screen, the robonurse began to talk. "We have screened the DNA and considered other relevant data, such as where you live, past offences, the achievements of ancestors, and so on. There is a ninety-two per cent chance that this human will cause a net deficit to the economy of four hundred thousand dollars over their lifetime."

Harrie gulped. That was an awful lot more than

she'd expected.

"Therefore, you have three options."

The human nurse clicked her fingers and took over. "I know it's difficult," she said. "A choice nobody wants to make, but you must."

Harrie was stony-faced, neither encouraging nor discouraging the nurse to continue.

"If you pay within thirty days, or an annual amount for the remainder of your life, your daughter will get full, free, and lifelong access to the welfare state. Alternatively, you can give permission for the clinic to terminate."

Harrie's shoulders caved and she held her head in her hands, denying the nurses a quick answer. The robonurse pressed for a decision, stating that, without a financial commitment, the default option was termination. Gradually, Harrie straightened until she was sitting at full height, her back erect and her eyes staring directly at the nurses.

"I'll crowdfund the four hundred thousand dollars."

"I'm afraid that is not possible," said the robonurse.

Harrie leapt up and smashed the palms of her sweaty hands against the screen, adding to the smeared scum already there. "Not possible? What do you mean, not possible?"

"New regulations. Making any financial information

public on any human of any age is illegal."

"New? Since when? Not at conception. Not enforceable."

Still and silent, the robonurse waited for an answer. Harrie stared at it.

Eventually, the robonurse broke the silence. "Default chosen."

The nurses left her to weep alone.

GATHERING POWER

Her cluster of friends had been hushed. Her connection implants dialled down as close to zero as possible. Her panel displays blurred. She glanced at the fridge, switched off in her determination to avoid an accidental alert to anyone outside her home. She relished the isolation stretching out in front of her, and yet at the same time she longed for someone to break her veneer of solitary contentment. She wanted to be alone and she wanted to be wanted. What someone had once inaccurately nicknamed Schrödinger's Friends.

She sat on her bed, flicking her head in rhythmic jerks, moving from one pointless piece of click-bait to the next, but despite the attempt to keep the darkness at bay, a crippling apathy for life enfolded her. She had a niggling feeling that something was wrong with her cluster buddy Jamie, but she pushed it to the back of her mind. She winked, she smiled, and she blew kisses to comments from the online acquaintances she stumbled across in her wanderings. Gestures as pointless as the posts they praised.

There was an irritating thump, thump, thump in the hallway. She strolled to the front door and turned the full-length panel to its viewing setting. Next door's kids were busy bouncing a ball against the wall. They waved. She switched the panel to one-way and watched them for ages. Until she got worried that they would start to appear on her day-to-day connections as proximities, mixed in with her chosen cluster. It was for that very reason she avoided too much flesh contact with anyone.

Each one of the implants scattered across her body represented a friend, a member of her cluster. A cluster initially drawn together around a shared obsession with the obscure art movement, Vorticism. She knew who was who by the implant's location and vaguely knew how they were feeling from the pattern of its vibrations. There was a beautiful harmony of frustration and comfort in being constantly aware that they were out there living their lives.

The implant that connected to Jamie was still worrying her. He was the only one from her cluster who lived close by and the only one she had flesh met, and he was struggling with something, but she couldn't summon the energy to find out what. It was selfish. She knew that. It was also about protecting herself from being swamped by whatever he had going on.

Back in her room, she listened to the kids playing. Now that she knew what it was, the steady thump of their ball was comforting and their occasional laughter made her smile. She felt more in tune with the world, and when Jamie's distress increased another notch, triggering her pre-set alarm settings, she dialled her panels up to full. He appeared on the nearby street where the windows of the shops selling repurposed tech doubled up as panels. Naked from the waist up, he was swaggering along unashamedly showing off his implants for anyone to see. God, he was sexy. It was brave, it was stupid, and it was typical of Jamie. Not the first time, and as ever likely to attract the wrong sort of attention. The display crystalised into a scene formed from snippets of those in her cluster. She loved how it pieced together someone in their kitchen, someone in the street, someone on a train, and so on, into a collage that made it look as if they were all in the same space. Ten of her fifty-strong cluster were waving and shouting greetings.

Jamie's distress—or was it excitement?—increased again.

"What's happening with Jamie?" she asked, hoping it wasn't another system glitch her body would misread and react to in some unnecessary way.

They ignored her and instead asked how she was, noting she'd been absent for a while. Some sent probing messages directly to her earbud asking how she "really" was and why her vitals were so off, especially her gut bacteria. She told them not to worry and that she'd been getting some alone time, to which they responded with messages of empathy tinged with concern. She was pleased. It was nice to see them again, and soothing to be reminded that they cared. She decided that Jamie's distress was most likely a sign of the adrenalin pumping around his body and relaxed into watching his promenade. Waiting for the inevitable.

Sure enough, a bunch of anti-cluster thugs appeared and surrounded him, threatening him with scalpels and offering to relieve him of his weirdo implants. He grinned as he dodged from side to side. Each time he came into view, he yelled for help.

"Shit. Why does he do this?" she muttered. "Call the police," she shouted.

Her friend Tilly shouted back. "Done!"

"Leave him alone!" she screamed at the thugs. Using the panel's latest feature, she told it to face-recognise them, and within seconds it displayed their names and addresses. "Look, you idiots," she shouted. "Look at the panel. We know who you are. Piss off or we will find you and—"

The thugs stopped and stared at the ten faces hurling abuse at them. They turned to each other, hesitated, then ran away shouting obscenities over their shoulders.

She was exhausted.

Back in bed with her panels blurred, she connected directly with a few friends and just chatted. She felt better after a few reassuring bouts of banter, and propping herself up with her pillows, she set her panels to a half-setting and relaxed. A day of having her cluster nearby without having to interact was what she had wanted, and was most likely what she had needed all along.

The doorbell rang. She pulled herself out of bed and ambled to the door. Jamie was there, topless, with a grin and a takeaway. She chuckled; he certainly knew how to press her buttons.

FAR SIDE WHISPERS

It has been the longest and loneliest night that I can remember. I know I chose to leave and set myself apart, but it hurts far more than I imagined and the intense pain of leaving Wang Lei is still raw. I'm hungry.

"I love you all," I whisper, setting a wave of parleparticles free to traverse the bleak terrain and find a welcoming ear among the community I turned my back on.

The tiny strip I've torn from my bubble tastes foul. It's losing its structure and not only that, the insides of my mouth itch as the last few parleparticles die. I need sunlight to arrive soon. I need regeneration.

I rest my head against the depleted fabric of the bubble, gazing past the edge of its protective cloud of breathable air and up to the stars. One day, I think. One day, I'll explore properly. With my finger I trace the intricate patterns the stars paint across the sky and my thoughts drift, soaked in the images conjured up by the myths and legends told about our ancestors. Of great walls built to separate us from the dangers we cannot see. Of warriors on beasts with four legs, fighting for a unifying peace. Of flying through the vast emptiness to settle on this, our home. There is much to remember and even more to be learnt.

The sun rises, and with its unsurpassed beauty it brings light and warmth. The bubble clicks as it regenerates. Renewing and growing again. Sucking up the bright rays of solar energy and becoming the lush source of shelter and food it was designed to be.

Hungrily, I rip chunks from the sides, the floor, and the roof. Shoving them into my mouth with such decadent abandon that any decent Lunarian would steer clear of me for fear of being tainted by my uncontrolled gluttony. If I were back in the Community of Common Destiny right now they'd still be ritually thanking their lucky star that the bryophyta-proxy was growing their bubbles again. And that's why I had to leave. Imagine such adherence to ancient and archaic practices. Not to mention sleeping all the way through the darkness and then staying awake through the whole of the sunlight. Never taking the time to see, let alone wonder at, the stars. No time to dream about adventures far away. It's enough to make you scream, but that's not what we do. That is *not* what we do.

I stretch to shake off the food and the night. I can only just touch the walls with my fingertips and then I can't. It's growing fast. It'll stop once it's reached the predestined size for single occupancy and only regenerate when I take pieces from it. I breathe in the rich aroma. The bubble has grown strong and thick. Transparent. I dig my fingers halfway into its flesh and tear a length for a bubbleblanket light enough for me to move around more freely. It feels good to rip. To not follow the ways of the CCD of carefully cutting a section of precise proportions. Freedom feels succulent beneath my fingernails. With the blanket engulfing and protecting me like the bubble, it's safe to step out of my home and into the day.

It doesn't take long to bounce to the edge of the lake and enter its own protective bubble. I kneel down and meditate on the faint ripples across its surface. Repeating our mantra over and over while the blanket soaks up liquid. "Life comes from where we do not know and returns to where we do not know."

Once the surface of the blanket has developed its

satiated sheen, I finish the mantra with the traditional communal entreaty, even though there's nobody to share it with. "A candle lights others and consumes itself."

I have tried to get the elders to reveal what this bizarre phrase means because the myths, legends, and songs are better at recounting facts, such as the ancients' mastery of artificial light on our planet of origin, than they are at explaining the philosophy they contain. The CCD response hasn't been particularly helpful. Something along the lines of: *trying to be the centre of attention will destroy you*. Whatever it may or may not mean, it's a comforting end to the ritual. Completing the circle of life, I've heard it called.

The mysterious whispers are strongest by the lake, in the absence of competing community whispers. They cling to my receptors, ebbing and flowing as if they are being blown out and sucked back. Slowly, I rotate until they are at their most intense. If I'm to find their source, that's the direction of travel to take. I turn back to the lake and listen for the distant whisper-hum of the CCD, who by now should be undertaking their own sunrise mantra a little way along the edge of the lake. It's not there. No sound of them. No whisperings. Inhaling the slight saltiness of the freshly invigorated blanket, I turn to face the vague yet strangely addictive whispers calling me to a different place. Chewing on a sliver of nutrition peeled from beside me, I lift my head and close my eyes. I wait. The whispers surround me, beckoning me forwards.

Bending my knees, I push hard against the barren ground and launch myself forward. The sooner I set off, the more likely it is that I will find their source before darkness returns. The bubbleblanket holds me tight and I bounce once, twice, three times and I'm away. The rocky surface feels spongy as I leap and land, compressing the blanket between my feet and the ground, while all the time the whispers call me towards them. I glance behind and gulp as I realise the lake is almost out of sight. I steady myself. Now I've started, I must carry on. I must make the most of the freedom I've snatched and go wherever it takes me.

As I bounce up and over the lip of our crater I'm confronted with a vast plain of barren land and I can't help thinking about the companionship the community offers and the control it imposes. Why, oh why, couldn't Wang Lei let go of them? How I wish he was making this journey with me, sharing the experience and making me feel safer than I do right now. What is it I feel? Exposed is the only word for it. Physically exposed to the elements, mentally exposed by severing the connection to the community, and spiritually exposed to the embrace of the whispers. I take a snack from my bubbleblanket and bounce forward as fast as I can.

Thousands of bounces later, and after many rests along the way, I come to a long and shallow crater. I falter at its edge then I slide down on my back into its basin, letting the air surrounding the blanket cushion me from the sharp rocks that litter the crater's sides. At the bottom, there's a perfectly cylindrical pipe about the height of my waist. It doesn't look natural. All of my indoctrination tells me to stay away, to avoid the unknown, but I bounce across to take a closer look, excited to follow my instincts and be free from CCD. It's hard to explain, but the whispers are getting more insistent. It's as if they want me to be here. To approach the pipe. One final bounce and I stumble to a halt next to it. Once again, the bubbleblanket protects my body as well as my breathing. Covering the pipe is a faint trace of what looks like the same bryophyta-proxy that forms the fabric of the blanket. As I touch the pipe, the whispers increase and the blanket hums. Something is calling from inside. What? Why? Where from? I bend my knees to make the leap onto the pipe. I push against the ground and land squarely on top. Daylight is fading the further I go from home, which is bad news for my blanket, but what can I do except continue? It can't be helped. I must press on, and press on I do. Getting into the rhythm of bending knees, pushing hard, and bouncing along the pipe faster and faster. Each leap is longer than the last. In my peripheral vision the pipe passes underneath, but I keep my eyes on the horizon. I must not fall.

At the end of the crater the whispers become almost unbearable. I pause to steady myself before attempting the slope upwards and notice a trickle of liquid leaking from the pipe onto the blanket, which is happily soaking it up. Amazing. Could this be where the liquid that fills the lake comes from? I push harder, bouncing up the slope and out of the crater. Ahead, where the pipe disappears, is a massive solid structure blocking my way, and it looks as if it's constructed from rocks. It stretches into the sky by at least ten times my height and appears to have no end to my left or my right. Up close it gets even weirder. The rocks are of uniform size and shape, placed one on top of another. I want to lean against it to see if it will withstand my weight, but I don't. Instead, I stroke it gently through a thin layer of blanket. The individual rock cubes that form the structure are surprisingly flat compared to the rocks on the ground and have a soft sheen to them. I've felt something similar to this warm mucus before. It's reminiscent of the outer membrane of the large bubble that covers the lake. Something sparkles. A flat piece of hard, cold material that I don't recognise is fixed to one of the cubes. It has writing on it: *The Second Great Wall*. Could it be one of the mythical walls? From the legends about Earth and Lunar? Two walls, visible to one another. Reminders of an ancient connection, severed when the Earth barbarians finally ceased their evil and focused on healing their home. Artificial steps similar to the natural ones on some of the craters are cut into the side of the structure. I might be able to use them to bounce to the top. There's just enough room to land the blanket on each of the steps. I'm going to try. Keeping my eyes firmly on my feet, I bounce more carefully than I've ever bounced in my life. I pause briefly between each one. Sweat pours from my face and from underneath my armpits. Some of it I'm sure is from the exertion of taking such care and some of it from sheer anxiety. I'm almost there, and as I make the final bounce, I check to make sure the top of the structure is wide enough for me to stand on. It is.

Wow!

What is that?

A large sphere with swirls across its surface is hanging in the sky. It's beautiful and shocking at the same time.

Wow!

It's not getting any closer. It's hanging there as if it belongs right where it is. Down in front of me it's dark, night-time, and yet there are pinpricks of light. Are they stars? Am I on the edge of my world, with another in the sky? On the horizon a blue glaze covers the ground, eerily lighting up the mountains and craters in the far distance. I pull my blanket tight and sit down. Staring at the orb and then the pinpricks beneath me. The whispering is intense, bombarding me from all sides. There's no structure to it that I can decipher. It's simply a disturbing dissonance. The blanket emits an acrid odour, warning that decay has begun. Forward or backward? Bounce off the edge into the unknown? Leap and hope it's not the edge of the world? Return to the lake, none the wiser? I don't know. The orb is incredibly wonderful. Too wonderful to ignore.

It's amazing.

The ground lights up with a bright red burst revealing a large oblong shape. What is it? What's happening? The oblong is hovering.

"Help. I need help."

The stones beneath me vibrate violently as the oblong repeatedly presses against the wall. I stare with my mouth wide open, breathing rapidly and stroking the inside of the blanket. I'm stunned and unable to think straight. And then it hits me as I recall one of the lakeside stories told as cautionary tales by the light of dusk. That one day, aliens from Earth would visit with their violence. What took me so long to realise? It's obvious. The whispers are an attempt to communicate. CCD needs to know. I have to warn them. I scratch the inside of my mouth to activate the dying parleparticles.

"Help," I whisper, in the hope it will reach CCD. "Help, help, help. Aliens are landing."

That's it. That's as much as I can whisper. All my parleparticles have been used up, and the blanket is decaying fast. It's too dangerous to strip enough food from it to be able to utter another whisper. I want one last long look at the orb before I leave. It's lush and enticing, but CCD has taught me well. Not everything is as it appears. I turn my back on the orb, risk tearing a small strip from the blanket to give me energy, and take the first bounce back towards the regenerating sunlight.

With all the effort I can muster, I bounce back down the wall faster than is safe, across to the crater, and slide down on my back with my legs pointing upwards. Inside the crater I bend and bounce with such force that I veer chaotically. I don't care. I hurtle across the barren plain at breakneck speed, oblivious to any danger, vaguely conscious that the blanket has stopped emitting its rancid smell. The faint sunlight is rejuvenating it. My body is aching from the exertion of not resting, but it's worth it. CCD and the precious lake are a long way away. I could rip pieces off the blanket and stuff them in my mouth, boosting my immediate energy and the bounces that come from it. I could attempt to find my community. But why? The chances are they'll have taken the opportunity of the long period of sunlight to migrate. It's not as if we've never done it before when there's been a trauma to the community. Presuming that's what my departure is. I'm going to be alone forever. The aliens are coming and I have to face them on my own. What if I wait here for them? I could embrace them, and whatever they bring. No. No, that's not a good idea. What should I do? Press on? Wander the lake looking for CCD? That's not a good idea either. The alien whispers are faint, and yet I can't get the oblong or the orb out of my mind. It was so beautiful hanging there in the sky like a big round rock covered in gigantic lakes. If I don't explore and find out more, I'll regret it until my dying day. CCD has another saying: *better to live a good day than a bad year.*

That's it. Decided.

I reunite my blanket with its larger self and get ready to begin the difficult bounce back inside my full-sized bubble. It'll be slower, but it'll be a lot safer when I'm back at the wall. One last goodbye whisper to my community, and I prepare to leave.

As I turn, a parleparticle reaches me, asking me to wait. I twist my shoulders and the bubble revolves until it faces the direction of the entreaty. It has the intonation of Wang Lei, heightening my hopes that he understands I am more than just another member of the Community of Common Destiny, and that he has rescinded his blind loyalty to them. He and I share a common destiny that is uniquely ours. A future of our own. I wait. The whisper gets stronger, but nobody appears. Waves of parleparticles reach me, exciting me and causing the membrane of my bubble to glisten. I catch the briefest of flashes from the direction of the lake. I strain my eyes, squinting to focus on the spot where it came from. It's too far away. The parleparticles grow stronger until at last I can see the shape of a bubble. It's Wang Lei. I can't make out the individual words, but I can tell from the lilt of the whisper and the formation of the bursts of language that it's him.

Finally, I hear him clearly. "Feng Mian," he whispers. "Wait."

"That is exactly what I am doing," I whisper back with my own parleparticle wave. "I'm waiting for you Wang Lei. I'm waiting for you to believe in me. In us."

It seems like forever as he makes his way towards me, giving me time to consider our future. He knows what I want. The joining of our bubbles into a family bubble, taking the risk that we might not be compatible and that our coming together might cause one of us to become sterile. But the rewards could be astronomical. Babies. New life. A mixture of him and me coming into existence, growing and developing until they move away into their own safe bubble with their own hope of partnering. It's the dream we all have. A dream that some will sacrifice their happiness for. A dream I hold on to on my own terms.

I hear him loud and clear. "Feng Mian," his parleparticle whispers. "Where have you been?"

I clumsily ask why he came looking for me, and he tells me that when I was no longer there, he realised that the risks of partnering with me without permission far outweighed the agony of my absence.

"Wang Lei," I whisper. "There's a blue orb with white swirls across its surface and patches of grey-brown beneath them. And an oblong. And a wall."

He bounces his bubble as close as is permitted, and I tell him about my visit to the wall and the aliens trying to knock down the Second Great Wall—which does exist, by the way.

"Show me the orb," he whispers into the silence that

punctuates the end of my story.

"And the oblong. We must warn CCD," I whisper.

"They won't listen."

"They must."

"They won't. You know they won't, but if I have seen it too then we can tell them together. Then they will take notice."

"Are we together?" I ask.

"Yes," he whispers. "We can perform the ceremony as soon as we return to CCD."

"Now," I whisper. "Without a ceremony. Let's combine."

He turns away and I wait, conscious that an interruption could send him the wrong way. My suggestion that we join our bubbles and forego the traditional words and chants that accompany such a momentous decision is radical, and I don't know whether he really is ready for me, irrespective of the consequences.

"Without the pre-ceremony tests they might not allow us to breed," he whispers. "I want a family with you."

"I want that as well," I whisper back. "I want it more than anything. Except you, I want you more than anything."

"Except your freedom," he whispers and grins.

I grin back. "Yes, except that."

He stares into the distance for ages. Not whispering. Not acknowledging me. Chewing slowly and deliberately on tiny strips torn carefully from his bubble. Every now and again, he moans emotional conflict. Finally, he turns to me and sends a sharp click of a whisper. I click back, relieved that he's made his decision.

We turn our bubbles away from the lake, and side by side we begin the journey back to the wall, the oblong, and the blue orb. His whispers are romantic and full of love, telling me how much he has missed me and that he has always known I was the one he wanted to try for a family with. He's less convincing when I press to see if he believes me about the aliens, but I'm comforted that he's willing to make the journey and see for himself. If he thinks I'm utterly delusional, he wouldn't be entertaining the notion of coupling, and I can live with that because when we get to the wall he'll see that I'm right. We bounce and bounce, gradually getting closer to each other as we get closer to our destination. It's much slower travelling in the bubbles compared to the blanket, but being with Wang Lei more than compensates for the frustration.

At the crater's edge, I drop to my back and slide down, and he follows. His whispers are somewhat erratic as he bumps and glides down to the floor of the basin. We pick ourselves up, and I prepare to bounce its length as fast as I can.

"Stop," he whispers.

"What?" I whisper back, not bothering to turn my head to face him.

"Now," he whispers.

I relax my tensed limbs, which were on the verge of launching me across the surface. "Now?"

"Let us couple."

"Here?"

"Here."

I've been waiting for this moment since we first exchanged whispers, but his timing could not be worse. "What about the orb and the oblong?" I ask.

"They will wait."

"I'm not so sure they will."

"We can be quick," he whispers with his most alluring intonation.

Quick. Hurried. Alone. It has a certain romance about it. A danger distanced by desire. I move my bubble next to his so they are touching and push my hand through the membrane, followed by the rest of my body. Arm then chest then right leg then left leg, finally pulling my buttocks through to join Wei Lang. Our bodies touch, and for the first time in my life I experience the sensation of the skin of another who is not my family. His bubble smells different to mine, and in time we will create our own unique smell. For a few moments we act out the part of the coupling ceremony, where the two raise their arms and place the palms of the hands together, then roll their arms against one another and then their chests, before turning around with bodies still touching to rub their backs. It is sensational, and for those moments I have no thoughts other than the smell and the touch of Wang Lei.

"Feng Mian," he whispers with such overwhelming eroticism that I stroke the bubble for a reminder of the familiar.

"Yes?"

"We must go," he whispers.

Clumsily at first, we bounce together in the newly formed bubble that has combined from our two single bubbles. Before long we are happily synchronised, and the double bounce doubles the pace of our progress. His soft, damp skin brushes against mine and his scent gets stronger as the perspiration from his pores increases. We hit an uneven piece of ground, the bubble tilts to my side, and he bumps into me. His hand rests on my stomach as he corrects his stance, and we bounce again. I can feel his handprint lingering on the surface of my skin and the tingling traces of it creeping up and across my breasts to my neck. I had no idea that sharing a bubble could be so full of pleasure. I wonder if my parents ever felt this, ever experienced this sensational thrill and the delight of each other's bodies. I quiver. He nudges my shoulder and grins.

"Up there," I whisper, pointing at the top of the slope out of the crater.

We half bounce, half stumble our way to the top, and there it is: the wall.

"Look," I whisper. "The Second Great Wall."

His mouth hangs open.

"Do you believe me now?"

"Yes." He takes hold of my hand. He's trembling. "On the other side?" he asks, his intonation oscillating in time with his body.

"Come and see," I whisper, tightening my grip on his hand to reassure him. "It is spectacular."

We rip off two bubbleblankets, and I notice that the pipe from the wall to the lake is leaking its whispering liquid, which is then seeping into the ground. The oblong is beginning to cause real damage. We must do something. We carefully bounce our way up the wall, me in front and Wang Lei close behind. His whispers are meant to make me less afraid, but all they really do is show how scared he is. The higher we go, the more violently the wall vibrates. The oblong must be continuing its rhythmic, pounding assault.

When we reach the top, I pull his blanket into mine to form a double and pull him tight to me. The blue orb hangs in the sky, giving the distant horizon the same blue sheen I saw earlier. His shaking slows and his whispers become full of awe and wonder. The oblong shoves itself against the rocks, and the wall shudders once more. As it moves away and then back against the wall, the red light underneath moves too, lighting up the base of the wall. Over and over again. Wang Lei is almost whimpering, and it makes me want him all the more. It's difficult to distinguish his whispers from the cacophony coming from the oblong and the surrounding pinpricks of light, which I had assumed were stars but now wonder if they are artificial.

"Beautiful," whispers Wang Lei as he stares at the blue orb.

"Look at the lakes," I whisper.

"I see. I believe you."

We stand wrapped in each other's arms, in amazement at the sight before us.

The wall shudders underneath our feet, but the spectacle in the sky is so fully absorbing that the vibrations retreat into the background and I'm barely aware of them. As I turn my face towards him, he does the same and I kiss his lips. This is the most magical of moments and I want to savour it forever. We stand

and smile at each other, reluctant to break the spell. The oblong rises towards us. It's no longer pounding. Silently and smoothly, it approaches. Its red light casts an ominous glow on the mucus covering the rocks that make up the wall. When it reaches us, a flat black surface slides out until it touches the edge and an aperture in the oblong opens. Two figures emerge, covered head to toe in close-fitting material with strange bulbous casings where their heads should be. On each casing is a red rectangle split in two with a big star and four smaller stars on one half and at least fifty tiny stars on the other. At their sides they hold objects the length of their legs. Wang Lei whispers a greeting to them, and they raise their hands to the side of their casings. They look at each other, and one of them taps the front of the casing where a mouth should be. The other slowly moves their casing from left to right and back again and then taps the hand holding the object. They both lift the objects so they are pointing at us, and the cacophony of whispers ceases. A single whisper comes from their direction. Repetition of short and long bursts. Flat and soulless. Meaningless. Once again, Wang Lei whispers greetings and I join in. We sing our song, the one we use to greet new life as it's born. They lean forward, one leg in front of the other, still pointing the objects at us. Two holes appear in the blanket above our heads, one at the front and one at the back.

The blanket rapidly repairs itself, but it won't be able to do that too many times.

"They mean us harm," whispers Wang Lei.

"Give them a chance," I whisper back, but as soon as I finish two more holes appear, this time closer to our heads.

The blanket repairs, but the odour of decay warns us of its imminent demise. We need to return to the rejuvenating sunlight, and we certainly cannot withstand another attack.

"Do you remember the ancient stories where those being attacked scream?" I whisper hurriedly.

"I do, and the silence that always follows as the tellers let us imagine what a scream sounds like. Are you suggesting?"

"I am. We have no choice."

"Agreed."

We each draw a breath deep down into our lungs and let out an almighty scream. We keep it going for as long as we can, watching the figures in front of us drop their weapons and clutch the sides of their heads. Wang Lei's screaming is the most painful thing I have ever endured. It sounds as if all the pain of a lifetime has been set loose in one excruciating moment, and

I'm sure it's the same for him hearing me. It's having the desired effect though. We look at each other and nod. We need to scream again no matter how much torment it causes us. We take a second deep breath and draw another screeching scream of pain from the depths of our souls. The figures turn and scramble across the black surface towards the oblong. They are almost at the opening when it wobbles and falls from the sky, taking them with it. At the same time all the lights that littered the ground on their side of the wall are extinguished, leaving only the orb and its blue haze. The whispers come to an abrupt end.

We stand and wait for the red light of the oblong to reappear, or for the pinpricks of light to return, or for the whispers to begin. While all the time the odour of the decaying blanket gets stronger. We hold each other close and watch and listen. Nothing happens. The darkness and the silence prevail.

A small shadow passes across the front of the orb and then vanishes.

"They've gone."

"I think they have," whispers Wang Lei. "We need to get home and warn CCD."

"Will they believe us?"

"I don't know. We have to try."

I turn and kiss him on the lips.

"I believe in you. I'm sorry I ever doubted," he whispers.

I split our blanket so we can descend the steps of the wall and return to the security of the community. We will face many questions about our unlawful coupling and the risks we have taken, but surely the enormity of our discovery and the disaster we have prevented, or at least delayed, will override their petty-minded punishment. Won't it? I hope so. Otherwise, we are banished and forever forgotten when all we are guilty of is satiating our curiosity and allowing our love to take its course. As I turn towards him, the wall cracks and a faint haze of dust appears above its surface. We freeze, unable to move. The cracks widen and my feet shift slightly apart, stretching the blanket so thinly I'm worried it'll snap. Wang Lei looks petrified. My legs are about to buckle. The rocks give way beneath us and we tumble down the wrong side of the collapsing wall, bumping and bouncing among the crumbling rocks until we come to a halt at the bottom. My blanket fills with the smell of decay. Looking up, I can see no way for us to get back to the top and over in the time we have left.

Wang Lei's whispers are incoherent.

I combine our blankets and gently stroke the back of his hand. His fear subsides and we are silent, staring at the blue orb and touching each other for comfort.

We are the expiring candles of our mantra, flickering farewell.

EXTRACTING HUMANITY

Sara heard the faint murmurings of an indistinct voice. It grew louder but no clearer. In a dreamy daze she opened her eyes, and reality hit her squarely in the face. Squatting opposite was her lover, her best friend and fellow resistance fighter. Head down, mumbling and absent-minded, Madeleine was carefully re-arranging the bleached bones of the innocent kitten that had been their last proper meal—this time into a hexagon-shaped pyramid. Sara had lost count of how many days it had been since the kitten, a few twigs, and an ember had been dumped on the dirty ground next to their wood pile. They had ignored the so-called gift, and then as the ember was dying and the hunger became unbearable, they caved in. Without speaking, Madeleine had taken care of building the fire and Sara had cut the kitten along its length with the only tool they were permitted, ripped it open and, through a veil of dusty tears, prepared it. Turned inside out and hung over the roaring flames, it had sizzled as its layer of fat had melted and dripped onto the burning wood. They both knew what they were doing. They both knew this nightmare could come to an end with a simple phrase uttered at the gate of the prison. All they had to say was "the rebellion is extinct", but they had refused once again to buckle. Ingesting the charred flesh of a fellow Earth dweller was a sacrifice worth making for the cause.

Sara was waking up slowly. The raindrops from the geo-engineered cloud above them became dark brown patches on the ground as they landed. The white bones of the pyramid momentarily darkened whenever a falling raindrop collided with the careful construction that kept Madeleine busy. "Morning," she said without looking up.

"Morning," replied Sara, her voice thick and sleepy. "Ohm," Sara added instinctively. She had uttered the symbol of resistance so many times that the call sign of the movement had lost its meaning unless she paused to contemplate its value.

"Ohm," replied Madeleine, again without looking up.

Sara studied her. She was beautiful. They'd never married, couldn't see the point. That was something they both now regretted. To face their final fate together would have made it tolerable, or so they told themselves, but as an unrecognised couple they would be separated when the time came. Madeleine's awkwardness made Sara's insides melt. There was a veneer of vulnerability that hid the granite core of this wonderful, principled woman perfectly. As if that wasn't enough, she had the most enthralling eyes and exquisitely shaped lips that simply drew you in, leaving you with no doubt that you had been well and truly captured. And Sara had been for the past five years, two of which had been spent in this prison of conscience designed to ram home the message that humanity dominated nature and any view to the contrary was treason.

"I'll see what I can find to eat," said Madeleine. She brushed her pyramid to one side, collapsing the carefully constructed bones into an untidy pile, and as she passed by she stooped down to stroke the growing bulge of Sara's pregnant body. "Not long now," she said with a sigh. The soft, sad tinge to her voice conveyed all she needed to convey about their situation.

The guards had arrived one afternoon, taken Sara away, and forcefully inseminated her with a fertilised egg, making it clear that this foetus was engineered to go full term and be born. But without advanced medical assistance, it would only live a single day. "You could always roast it on the second day while it's nice and fresh," one of the guards had joked as they delivered Sara back to her allocated space. Madeleine's response was to spit in the guard's face, which earned her five days' isolation and separation from Sara at the very time Sara needed her most.

Sara contemplated those long, lonely days while she watched Madeleine finding them food. She watched her stoop and pick, stoop and pick. When Madeleine returned she had a few dandelion leaves, some nettles, and a wild onion. She shrugged. They both knew that the inability to grow vegetables wasn't because nature was incapable, as the guards kept insisting. It was because the soil had been stripped of any life by the same chemically aided, genetically enhanced crops the guards now kept inside their fenced garden. She sat down next to Sara and cuddled in close. "All for you," she said as she handed Sara the fruits of her foraging. "Junior needs it more than me."

"You can't—"

Madeleine kissed Sara on the lips, swallowing the words of opposition before they could really form. The baby kicked and they both smiled. "She'll be a feisty one, that's for sure," said Madeleine.

"For a day."

They sat in silence, lost in their own thoughts.

Sara groaned. "Have they won?"

Madeleine cupped her hands around the unborn child inside her swollen lover. "Not yet," she said. "Not yet."

"I can't watch her die," whispered Sara. "You know they won't take her away when she dies, don't you? You know they'll starve us in the hope we *will* eat her?"

"They're not that cruel," said Madeleine.

"Don't be so sure," whispered Sara.

"We can bury her if she doesn't survive. They're probably lying about the genetic modification anyway, just to turn the screws some more. They'll do anything to crush us."

Sara ate her breakfast and Madeleine rebuilt her pyramid, both abandoned to their own thoughts and their own demons.

A siren sounded. It was time for another reminder that humanity was in control. The fierce sun burst through the edges of the clouds as they parted like curtains manipulated from behind the scenes. The heat intensified, and there was no choice but to find what little shelter they could in the shade of the fence posts that surrounded the guards' garden. It was especially cruel to be forced to sit within sight and smell of the bountiful treasure that lay beyond their reach. Once upon a time they would have refused such food, repelled by the artificial nature of its genetics, but Sara wasn't so sure they'd do the same now after so many months of starvation and subjugation. They were almost beaten.

As the sun moved across the sky, they moved with it from one fence post to another, always at least a post apart. Without warning, and as far as Sara could tell for no reason other than they could, the guards sounded the siren again and the clouds closed. The day was done, the point had been made, and it was back to cold and hunger.

At their allotted space they lay down next to each other and dozed the day away, tired, hungry, and sad. The baby kicked and they hugged. The rain fell and they curled up closer to each other. Madeleine did her best to protect Sara from the worst of the dampness. Darkness came eventually, and for a few hours the ground warmed from beneath. Another engineered alteration to a natural world. The warmth was bittersweet, as it was intended to be. It was welcome and despised at the same time. Adding to the erosion of their resistance, it pushed them one step nearer to the words they hoped they would never utter—the words that would signal an end to their resistance. The acknowledgement of their defeat would be broadcast to the watching world, dragging a deep scar across the hope they had created.

Madeleine dozed off, and Sara lay awake next to the sleeping woman who was her life. She wriggled free from Madeleine's embrace, stretched her legs, and stood over her lover, wallowing in her beauty and emotionally swallowing the memory for safekeeping. She clenched her jaw and squeezed her eyes tight. She had decided to leave the prison for the sake of her unborn daughter. Madeleine slept on, quietly snuffling as Sara walked away. The snuffle grew softer and more distant with every step until Sara could hear it no more. She didn't turn around to take a final look. Instead, she focused on the gate, clenched her fists, and walked as fast as she could.

At the gate, she dropped to her knees as they'd been told they must do when the exit from the prison had been explained on their arrival. "One day," the warden had said. "One day you will see the error of your ways and you will come to this gate, and on your knees you will admit that you were wrong and you will admit defeat in front of the world." He had pointed to the phrase etched into a plaque next to the gate that read: *The Rebellion Is Extinct*. "You will repeat the words from that plaque, saying nothing more and nothing less. Then you will be free. A truly free human being, no longer tainted by your idiotic notions."

Sara bent her neck upwards so that she was looking at the plaque, bit her bottom lip, and prepared to lose Madeleine forever.

She drew a deep breath and began. "The rebellion—"

She stopped. She couldn't say it. She placed her hand on her belly and said sorry. Sorry for being weak, sorry for the world into which the baby would be born, and sorry for being stupid enough to get captured and placed in this prison. "I'm not a traitor," she repeated under her breath over and over. "I'm not a traitor, and I never will be." She sobbed and the tears flowed freely. She was trapped. She was unable to return to the comfort of Madeleine and unable to leave her behind. So she knelt and cried, wailing into the manufactured night air, and it was while she knelt there that the guards came and collected her. They anesthetised her, undid her shirt, and pulled down her trousers. As she drifted away she saw them grinning.

When she came round, she was holding a small bundle of newborn baby. Anger boiled up inside. It was anger at the forced extraction of her baby and anger at the presumed moral superiority that gave them the right to dig into her reproductive system.

This was the same arrogance that continued to extract the innards of Mother Earth. Her daughter gurgled and Sara drew her close. She spat at the guard nearest her. "You have no right," she said.

The guard smirked. "It's you that has no rights," she said, more to her audience of other guards than to Sara. "On your way," she said and leveraged Sara off the bed and onto her feet. "Back to your comrade you go."

Full of rapid-recovery drugs, Sara stumbled out into the night. The only sound was her daughter snuffling away in her arms. She reminded Sara of curtains swishing back and forth, which brought the engineered clouds to mind and the bigger, more sinister issue of the geo-engineered world that her daughter had just inherited, briefly. Taking tiny, painful steps, she walked silently across the prison grounds to her lover.

Madeleine was still asleep, as beautiful as when Sara had left her. She nudged her sleeping lover, who sat bolt upright, ready to fight, trained by years of active rebellion to never fully relax. Sara held out the bundle of baby, and Madeleine accepted it with a twinkle in her eye.

"You did this alone?" she asked.

"They forcefully extracted her from me," said Sara.

"Bastards," said Madeleine, but quickly turned her attention to their daughter. "She's a fighter alright," she said. "Have you named her?"

"Carla. My warrior woman."

"Perfect. Hello, Carla," said Madeleine, holding Carla high in her outstretched arms towards the rising sun. "Look, they opened the clouds just for you. They don't do that every morning, you know."

That day was a long day and a day like no other. They held each other and they held Carla. They didn't cower in the narrow strips of shade from the fence posts. Instead, they lay in the baking heat for as long as they felt that Carla could endure it, or until she began wailing, coughing, or sneezing. They walked her around the prison grounds, took her to see the guards' garden and drew shapes by pointing at the sky and carefully tracing the outline of kittens and puppies in the folds of the grey and white cloud. They tickled her, they kissed her, and they held her tight. They needed to burn the memories of this precious day as deeply and permanently as possible. The guards brought some pale liquid, keen to convince Sara that it was a healthy baby brew. And, as Madeleine pointed out once the guards had gone, there was no real choice but to trust them if they were going to feed Carla anything at all. Night-time came, and they settled down next to their burnt-out pit of ash, waiting for the inevitable death that would come with the morning sunrise. They took turns holding her, neither of them sleeping a wink. They rocked her and sang to her the songs of the rebellion and the lullabies of their childhood, often with long pauses in between when they simply held hands and indulged in a light kiss without taking their eyes off their precious Carla.

The sky grew lighter. Sara and Madeleine grew darker. An orange glow flickered into being and slowly, but as surely as Carla's fate was sealed, the sun rose. They formed a basket of human hands and held Carla as if offering her to some unnamed and unknown god. Carla gurgled, oblivious to the impending end of her short life.

The sun rose, but nothing happened. The siren sounded and the cloud curtains closed. Another day was born without snuffing out human life. They couldn't fathom what to do. Both of them worried that if they relaxed, then Carla would be taken from them—either by her genetic programming switching something on or by switching something off, whichever method of termination had been used.

They sat and waited.

The guards came with another bottle of pale liquid. Sara kept quiet for fear of reminding them that Carla was supposed to die and shot a withering look at Madeleine as she began to speak. The guards left, and once more they fell into silence. Not the comfortable silence of two lovers enjoying a peaceful moment, but the silence of two petrified women unsure of the future.

They spent the day in much the same way as the previous one, but with a forced happiness and an edge of sadness. All the excitement had evaporated.

As the sun set, the cloud curtain opened and still Carla lived.

Sara fed Carla the last dregs from the bottle and rocked her to sleep. "You might as well sleep too," she said to Madeleine.

"Why don't I grab a couple of hours, and then you can wake me and we'll swap?" said Madeleine, twiddling Carla's left foot.

"Good idea. Sweet dreams," said Sara. She kissed Madeleine on the nose.

Madeleine chuckled. "We're getting a bit too babyish, aren't we?" she said.

Sara blew her a kiss and whispered, "Get some sleep."

Her two most precious people in the world were there, snoozing happily. It should have been a perfect moment, another to sear into the memory box, but it wasn't. She couldn't have them both, of that she was sure. During the day they'd had a brief but serious discussion about leaving, and Madeleine had been very clear that she would not yield and that the fate of the planet far outweighed the fate of one human being. Sara disagreed, convinced that the fate of the human race was entirely predicated on how we choose to protect the weakest individual. Madeleine thought it was a matter of priorities. Sara agreed.

Sara carefully collected Carla into her arms, kissed Madeleine lightly on the top of her head, and walked towards the gate.

She would kneel, and she would declare the rebellion extinct.

She would not yield her innocent daughter.

AFTERWORD

I love writing short fiction because of the way you can neatly package an idea into a burst of imagination. I discovered this while writing my second novel, *Fluence*, using it as a way to keep "bright ideas" out of the novel they didn't belong in, and I've continued to write long and short pieces in parallel ever since.

I've been extremely fortunate to work with scientists and technologists on projects designed to use near-future fiction to raise pertinent questions about where their research and innovations might take us— for better or worse. While only seven of the stories here are a direct result of these projects, the significant amount of background research they have provided pervades all my work, influencing the perspectives I bring to my writing.

I consider myself a bit of a skimmer and scavenger. However, it's vital to get a true, albeit lay-person, understanding of the science rather than relying on news stories which can be alarmist and even wrong. Collaboration is key, and gives me the opportunity to push the limits of the possible and the plausible in the knowledge that the experts I'm working with can validate or veto it. The great thing about these projects is that they produce work that sits in that grey area between utopia and dystopia because, through the process of working together, the scientists and by implication the science are humanised rather than demonised. This reduces the tendency to be entirely dystopian.

Rather than list a direct correlation between project and story, I'll give some examples of things I've been involved in and let you decide where the influences lie. One of these has been a project with King's College London, which is piloting development of an automated approach to coding expressed emotion in mothers' speech to improve prediction of youth mental health problems. Another that has stayed with me for the past five years was a symposium on human brain organoids and other novel entities at Oxford University by the International Neuroethics Society. This day of discovery and discussion continues to influence my writing. The work with the think-tank Cybersalon on a series of interdisciplinary, technology and policy investigations through science fiction storytelling, looking at the future of healthcare, the high street, community and money, has also been extremely informative. Finally, I worked with Furtherfield on their Citizens SciFi project to celebrate 150 years of Finsbury Park by collaborating with local residents, scientists, and technologists to consider the locality's future.

As I was putting this collection together, I began to wonder if science fiction has any influence on the future, and if it does, what my responsibilities as a writer are. At the same time I was asked to guest-edit an issue of Vector, the British Science Fiction Association's critical journal. I brought these two things together and the resulting issue, published in Spring 2023, has helped me answer that question.

To quote myself from Vector:

"Yes, speculative fiction does influence scientists and technologists in what and how they research, discover, and invent. Yes, its predictions do affect the future if you take 'predictions' and 'affect' in their broadest sense. To an extent, it has a responsibility to be accurate and not sensational, but shouldn't lose the 'attractiveness' of the story because then it'll be ignored. It doesn't have to be tech-utopian. For example, I want to warn and inspire, but not demoralise. At the very least, it should generate some action, even if that's only in subtle shifts of understanding and behaviour. And, although the primary purpose of speculative fiction is entertainment, don't forget that pondering possible futures can also be entertaining.

"Finally, to consider our futures through speculative fiction effectively we should avoid using individual stories as a prediction, but rather get a sense from a wide range of stories about the possibilities of where we might be heading, and what we might do about it.

"I want to end with supercharged activism, the fourth approach to applied science fiction described by Jo and Polina in Torque Control. Having often been on the 'fringe of the fringes' with one foot on the 'outside' and one on the 'inside' of the mainstream, this is an incredibly attractive notion. After all, the future is ours and it's up for grabs. So, let's give it a nudge in the right direction."

I hope you found the stories in this collection entertaining and thought-provoking, and enjoyed reading them as much as I enjoyed writing them.

ACKNOWLEDGEMENTS

Naturally, there are loads of people that deserve some acknowledgment for the forming of this collection, too many to include here. So, to name a few, there are those who asked me to work with them on projects. They are King's College London, most notably Christine Aicardi, Cybersalon, the artist Hallidonto, Cognitive Sensations, and Furtherfield. When it comes to my short story writing, Allen Ashley who runs Clockhouse London Writers deserves a mention, as do my beta readers—Penn, Jane, Paul, and Jared. I should also give a shout out to Ben Greenaway for his advice and insights into technology and to Luke Robert Mason's FUTURES Podcast for the inspiration it has provided. Finally, of course, a huge thank you to Orchid's Lantern for having faith in this collection.

ABOUT THE AUTHOR

Stephen Oram writes near-future science fiction. He has two published novels and is published in many anthologies, including the *Best of British Science Fiction 2020* and *2022*. He also works with scientists and technologists to explore possible futures through short stories, has co-edited three anthologies along these lines, and guest-edited the "Futures" issue of the BSFA critical journal, Vector.

Stephen is based in the heart of central London and attributes much of the urban grittiness and the optimism about humanity in his writing to the noise, the bustle, and the diverse community of where he lives.

Also by Stephen Oram:

Quantum Confessions
Fluence
Eating Robots and Other Stories
Biohacked & Begging and Other Stories

Printed in Great Britain
by Amazon